Lynne Markham

The idea for this book came to me when I saw the sad news reels of Moby, the sperm whale who took a wrong turning a few years ago. At the same time as this drama was being played out on the television a friend of mine suffered a severe stroke.

It seemed to me that to be trapped in a terrible situation with your intellect unimpaired, but without the power to communicate effectively, must be one of the cruellest of conditions.

In writing the book I tried to explore not only the feelings of isolation and frustration that ensue, but also some of the rewards, such as a greater awareness of others and our relationship to each other.

A whale, as one of the most civilised creatures on the planet, I thought to be a truly noble partner in this journey of exploration.

Also by Lynne Markham

The Closing March
Finding Billy

For younger readers

Lionheart
Winter Wolf

Contents

Deep Trouble

Lynne Markham

mammoth

Acknowledgements
I would like to thank Dr Keith Todd for his expert information on whale rescue missions. I would also like to thank the children and staff of Mapperley Plains Primary School for kindly allowing me to be a child for a day, and the staff of Beeston Ward at Nottingham City Hospital for generously giving me so much of their time.

First published in Great Britain in 2000 by Mammoth,
an imprint of Egmont Children's Books Limited,
a division of Egmont Holding Limited
239 Kensington High Street, London W8 6SA

ISBN 0 7497 4131 7

A CIP catalogue record for this book is available from the British Library

Typeset by Avon DataSet Ltd, Bidford on Avon B50 4JH
Printed in Great Britain by Cox & Wyman Ltd, Reading, Berkshire

For Sheila M. J.

Contents

1	Deep trouble	1
2	Dad's stroke	9
3	The whale	16
4	'Everyone knows he's going to die'	22
5	Fighting with Deep	25
6	Bashing Barker	34
7	'Your dad's still your dad'	39
8	Dad and me	44
9	'Jimmy Wilson is a wimp'	53
10	'Wake up, Deep!'	58
11	Waking Dad	62
12	Deep's decision	66
13	'I'm going to do something fantastic, Dad'	72
14	'Deep! Deep! Keep going, mate!'	81
15	'Starry, starry night'	88
16	'Sometimes whales will choose to die'	95
17	Tickling newts	100
18	'All at once he started to cry'	105
19	Bimbly glove	114
20	'You're a great bloke, Jimmy'	122
21	The big surprise	132
22	A change for the good	140

23 The greenhouse 147
24 'Good old Ben' 156
25 The great newt race 162
26 Celebrities! 168
27 Free at last 179

1
Deep trouble

The day the whale came to Bigsbury was the day everything went wrong. For a start, I got a red card at school for being late and then cheeking Miss Gray. I didn't mean to cheek her, I was upset because of Barker. So when she said, 'Jimmy Wilson, you are *late*!' with her eyebrows up and everybody looking and giggling and nudging each other, I just said, 'I don't care, right? Leave me alone!' and sat down at my desk and tried not to cry. The next thing that happens is: *slam*! A red card arriving in front of me, and that means I have to go and see the Head.

For a second start there was Barker. Barker spotted me in the playground reading a book and not taking much notice of anything else. And as soon as he spots me he comes right up and puts his head in front of my face and says, 'Wotcher reading?'

'Nothing,' I said, nonchalantly.

But my heart's going *bump* inside my chest because Barker's big and he's ugly. He'll bash you one as soon as look, so you *don't* look, and you hope he won't notice you. Only now Barker's in front of me, and there's my mate Ben scrunching his face up in sympathy but keeping away because he's scared of Barker the same as all the other kids are.

After that Barker snatches the book off me and says, 'This is about stupid animals, right? It's the sort of book a wimp reads.' Then he holds the book up over his head and lets it drop down on to the playground *smack* into a dirty great puddle. When I bend down to pick it up he gives me a kick so I fall in the puddle and splashes of mud fly everywhere. *That* means I have to go and get cleaned up, and *that* means I'm late and get the red card. And later on there'll be trouble with Mam when she sees what happened to my new school shirt.

Only that trouble never comes, because when I get home there's even worse trouble waiting. The third start. The sort of trouble you couldn't imagine unless it happened to you.

I got home from school with scruffy clothes and the red card and my book still wet, and our mam was already at home. I knew she was home as soon as I opened the door because I could smell oranges and bananas, and there were some grapes going brown in a bag on the table. Mam works in a greengrocer's and she gets to bring home the stuff they can't sell. It's a perk, right? One of the good things about the job, especially if you like fruit and veg. One of the bad things about it is that Mam talks fruit and veg nearly all the time.

Most of the time you don't even listen, but that day I listened because it was quiet. I went through the kitchen door and smelt the oranges and bananas, but Mam wasn't there. She didn't shout from the other room, either. Usually when I come in she'll give this yell: 'How-do, Jimmy! Will you have a banana? Class 1 Canary. Can't do better.' But that day there was an eerie quiet.

I put my bag down and picked up an orange and decided what to say about my shirt: 'I slipped, right? An accident.'

Or maybe: 'Me and Barker, we had a fight. You should see *his* shirt if you think mine's bad. I had to give him a bloody nose.' I could say that and just shrug a bit and stroll away like I didn't care.

Or maybe I could tell the truth: 'Barker took my book and knocked me down.' Only then she might just go up to school and everyone would see her and know, and Barker would still be hanging about.

I was mulling it over and noticing the quiet when the back door opened and Mrs Pidgeon came in. Mrs Pidgeon lives next door to us; she's joined on to the left-hand side and her house has these lions on the step by the door. Not real lions; lions made out of some black stuff that blows about when the wind's off the sea. The lions have got these stupid expressions, kind of scowling and bad tempered, but

Mrs Pidgeon's dead fond of them and gives them names like George and Henry, and polishes them all the time.

'Jimmy!' she says when she sees me there (Mam says Mrs Pidgeon's la-di-da), 'I was hoping your sisters might come home first. I saw the light, that's why I came. Your mother rang me, only now . . . I don't know. It's hard to tell you . . . I don't know if I should . . . but. Well then, Jimmy . . .' She sits down with a thump on one of the chairs, the one with the really wonky leg, and clasps her hands together tight. On each of her fingers there's a ring glinting. Four of them in a winking row. She carries on, 'I'm afraid your father's had an accident. Your mother's at the hospital with him now. I'll stay with you until your sisters get home from school, and perhaps they'll manage to give you your tea.'

Mrs Pidgeon's someone who doesn't like children, and in particular she doesn't like me. She always talks like I'm a nuisance somehow, and she avoids me if she sees me outside. But when she said that about Dad I just stared at her and imagined him slipping on a polished floor, or a vacuum cleaner running over his toes, or him breaking a glass and cutting his hand. That's the main thing I imagined. I couldn't picture anything else, unless he'd had a crash in the van.

'Has he broken his leg?' I said out loud.

And Mrs Pidgeon creaked on her chair. 'What?' she said. 'No, dear. Nothing like that.' Her eyebrows were drawn on like surprised brown semi-circles, so she couldn't frown if she wanted to.

'Well, what then? Did he get cut when he was washing up? Or did he fall off a ladder and hurt himself?' I didn't ask if he'd crashed the van, because that was the worst picture in my mind.

The eyebrows stayed up in two high, thin lines, and Mrs Pidgeon said nervously, 'No! Not that! I don't know what the trouble is. When your mother gets home, or your sisters are here . . . Your mother will explain it all, I'm sure.'

Mrs Pidgeon didn't say anything else in case it meant talking about our dad's job. She thinks we're funny because of what Dad does and she tries not to mention it out loud. She'll go, 'Your father's at business today, is he, Jimmy?' or 'Not everyone likes office work,' when what she means is, why doesn't he have a proper job like Mr Pidgeon? Mr Pidgeon works for the Water Board, though not in the office like Mrs P. says. He goes out with a tube that he listens through, so he can tell if a pipe is starting to leak.

And what's so special about mending pipes?

Nothing, that's what. And here's what I think: I think Dad is GREAT! And so do Mam and Madeline; it's only Chrissy who gets embarrassed when people mention about Dad's work.

Dad cleans people's houses and he's got a smart white van with DIRT BUSTER written on the side. Underneath that it says, *Leave it to me while you go out to work,* and that's the job he's been doing for over a year, ever since his business went bust.

Before he was a cleaner Dad made sandwiches, and he had a proper sandwich bar of his own, but he says the bottom fell out of that and there weren't any other jobs for miles around. Then Dad had a think and he remembered something: he did all the cleaning while our mam was out. He remembered as well that he *liked* cleaning and there was nothing he couldn't polish to a really great shine. So he put this advert in the *Evening Post*: CLEANING PERSON AVAILABLE. NO JOB TOO SMALL. But when the phone rang people were disappointed. They'd say, 'Oh no, Mr Wilson, I couldn't have that,' because other people are like Mrs Pidgeon; they don't think it's right to have a man clean their house. But he gets one job suddenly, and then another, and *bingo*! Our dad's everywhere. Ladies are ringing him all the time and some of them even stop Mam in the street. They try to get her to put a word in for them because everyone knows now how good Dad is.

Anyway, I was sitting looking at Mrs Pidgeon and she was trying not to look at me, when the door flew open and Chrissy came in. She saw me sitting with my arms folded and this funny hush like you get in a church. Mrs Pidgeon was opposite me, sitting dead straight with her hands in her lap and her face like a black rolled-up umbrella. And straight away Chrissy shot me a look. 'What's up? Where's Mam? Has our Jimmy done something he shouldn't?'

Mrs Pidgeon unrolled herself so her bracelets clanked on the table top. She said, 'Oh no, my dear. Nothing like that. I'm afraid your mother's at the hospital. Your father's had an accident, I'm sorry to have to tell you, my dear.'

'What sort of accident? What do you mean?' Chrissy put her bag down on the table and shook the hair out of her face. Then she stared dead hard at Mrs Pidgeon. 'Has he fallen off something, or cut himself?' (It's funny the way Chrissy thinks like me.) 'Or did he crash the van? Is that what it is?'

When Chrissy said that we both gave a gasp, as if something had slipped out of us by accident and we wished we could take it back. For a second or two afterwards there was this hush again, so we could hear the kitchen clock ticking and noises on the road outside. Then Mrs Pidgeon got slowly up. She said, 'I'm sure it's not as bad as that. This is the number of the hospital, dear. Why don't you give them a ring right now?'

Mrs Pidgeon put a piece of paper down on the table, and that's most of what I can remember. I don't remember her leaving, or Chrissy ringing the hospital, or even our Maddy coming home. What happened next is all mixed up like stuff you get in Mam's blending machine. There's colours, like Chrissy's dead-white face and the yellow splodge the light made on the scruffy kitchen floor.

And there's sounds. Our Chrissy saying into the phone, 'A *stroke*? What – *Dad*? You're wrong, Mam, you must be, he's not an old man.'

Then Maddy saying to me, very gently, 'You stay at home, pet, and have your tea. Me and Chrissy'll go to the hospital.'

And me saying, 'Yeah. Sure. OK.'

Only, not staying in but going out. Running off into the freezing dusk. My feet going clunk on the cobblestones and coming out on to the scruffy harbour and standing there looking at the black sloppy waves.

I was standing there, just looking, deliberately not thinking about Dad, but listening to the noise the waves made and the traffic going past high up on the bridge, when suddenly I saw something. Something huge and black rising up out of the water. I saw it hover there for a second or two like the hulk of a massive ship, then slowly, slowly go down again. A spray of water squirted up. You could hear the noise it made: *Grrr*! *Grrr*! Like a snore only bigger and louder than that. And then there was nothing. Except if you looked real hard you thought you could see an enormous shape, like the water was blacker and deeper in parts.

The shape you saw was the shape of a whale.

It was the day the whale came to Bigsbury.

2
Dad's stroke

The next day I thought I'd dreamt the whale. I thought it had swum into my head while I was asleep and filled it with its great black bulk and then slowly drifted out again.

I was crying when I woke up because I thought I'd lost something and I didn't know what, but I was scared I wouldn't get it back again. It was Saturday, and dead quiet when I went downstairs, not just because our dad wasn't there (he's usually not there on Saturdays because he does Mrs Piggot's ironing then) but quiet because Mam and Chrissy and Madeline weren't talking and the radio wasn't on.

Mam looked up when I went in the kitchen. She said, 'There's grapefruit for breakfast. Cape. The best.' And Chrissy got up and put an arm round me, so I knew things must be bad. Mam and the others looked like *they'd* been crying. Maddy's nose was running and her eyes were pink.

She kept dabbing at them with a handkerchief and then rolling the hanky into a ball. Chrissy's face looked red and white, the way it did when our budgie died. When I sat down next to her she took my hand and I couldn't rightly get it away.

Then I said, 'When will Dad be coming back home?'

And Chrissy snatched her hand back quick as a flash and said, 'Well, *honestly,* Jimmy, what a question to ask! Dad's had a *stroke*. That's pretty bad. He won't be home for ages yet.'

'Leave him, Chrissy, he's just a kid.' That was Madeline speaking up, and it made me say,

'What's a stroke, anyway?'

See, I pictured a stroke like next-door's cat. Not something to cry over, but something warm and soft under your fingers, and I knew I'd somehow got it wrong. The trouble was, I needed to know, because if I didn't, I might keep saying daft things and getting our Chrissy all het up.

But when I asked the question two things happened: number one, Chrissy kicked me hard under the table, and number two, Mam plopped her cup down with a bang and put a hand up to her mouth. For a long moment nobody spoke; there was just my leg going *throb* under the table and Chrissy glaring at me again.

Then Mam said, 'A stroke's what happens when a blood clot forms and you don't get enough blood through to your brain. Your brain gets damaged, Jimmy, love. It can't do what you want it to do, and that's what's happened to your dad. Your dad can't walk at the moment, pet, or move his arm, or even talk.'

When Mam said that Maddy gave this sob – *huh-huh* – into her handkerchief, and that set Chrissy off crying as well, and then our mam, and then I started up. We cried like we'd never done it before and we might have gone on crying if the phone hadn't rung.

When it rang we all stopped still and listened to the ringing noise, and then the answerphone clicking on and Dad's voice booming into the room: 'I'm sorry I can't take your call right now, but if you leave a message after the tone I'll make sure and get back to you as soon as I can.'

After that there was a strangled burp and then a funny high-pitched squeak, and then Mrs Piggot speaking out: 'Hello? Hello? I hate these things. Now where's my specs? Are you there, Raymond? You're not usually late, only Mr Piggot's been heavy on shirts and we've got our Sandra staying this week . . . And you know about *her*! I mean difficult! Everything washed and ironed every day. And particular . . . ! Well, I don't have to tell *you*! You'll be here then, will you? Soon as you can? Thank you, Raymond. Er . . . Goodbye.'

Her phone went down and ours rang again: 'Raymond? Raymond? This is Mary Stokes. About yesterday: where were you? Smokey's been sick on the living-room carpet and the kitchen needs more than a bit of a do. So, will you give me a ring? As soon as you can? Thanks, Raymond. Hope you're OK.'

After that a lot of things happened together. Maddy said, 'I'd better start ringing our dad's clients. Does he keep a list, Mam, d'you know?'

Mam said, 'It's in the van on Cranmer Street.' Then put a hand up to her mouth again.

Chrissy said, 'Right then, Mam, I'm coming with you to the hospital – and, Jimmy, make yourself useful just for a change. There's dusting to do and some spuds to peel, and I expect your room's in its usual state – so look sharp, will you? Don't just sit, and we'll see you when we get back home.'

They all got up from the table at once, so that suddenly the room was full. There was hair flying out and scarves getting tossed and Mam fussing over bags of fruit.

Maddy tried to put some lipstick on, and Chrissy said, 'Fancy you bothering about that now,' so Maddy blushed and shrugged her shoulders, and our Mam said,

'That's all right, love, you carry on. We have to try and act normally.'

When Mam stood up she looked different somehow, thinner and more bent, as if she had shrivelled like one of her plums. She went to the door and opened it, and then changed her mind and came up behind the chair where I sat. Both of her arms went round my neck and she whispered to me, 'Don't you worry, love. We'll soon get your dad back on his feet. You can go and see him in a day or two, but for now he has to sleep a lot.'

After they'd gone I stayed where I was, just staring at some empty cups and wishing I was somewhere else, a long way off form Bigsbury – London, say, or Birmingham. If you want to know, I felt left out. I felt like Dad was not my dad any more but someone I didn't really know; a stranger who you shouldn't ask questions about. And the house felt funny again; weird and too quiet. I kept getting this feeling again, like I'd lost something. Not a sock or a shoe or stuff like that. More as if a part of myself that you couldn't ever see or touch had mysteriously disappeared.

Then in my head I saw the whale moving very slowly out of the water. I saw it hover like a great torpedo, but beautiful and more grand than that, then slowly sink back down.

If it was a whale, I imagined it. Even last night when it came in my dream, I dreamt it as a whale, but I knew that it wasn't. I knew that it was really a seal and it was only a whale because I wanted it to be. I wanted to believe that I'd seen something that other people hadn't; something wild and splendid and free.

Perhaps it was thinking about the whale that made me

jumpy. The pots needed washing, my bed wasn't made, and I could nearly hear Chrissy saying to me, 'You're useless, our Jimmy. What are you?' but that didn't change the way I felt. Since yesterday, everything seemed different and not quite right, so in the end I made up my mind.

I put my coat on and went outside. There was a sharp wind blowing off the estuary. In next door's garden the two black lions had been blown over and were lying in a puddle with their feet in the air and their faces still wearing their stupid scowl. I went down our road and through the alley-way and past the baker's on Hargreaves Road, and I heard someone say, 'Hello there, Jimmy. Are you going to see the whale?'

And up until then I'd been walking, not slow but not fast, either. It's only when I heard those words that my legs started going faster and faster, like I was running some sort of stupid race; my head went back and my elbows came out. People had to scurry to get out of my way and I heard a lady say, 'Now then, pet,' but I was past her before she'd finished the 'pet' and on to the jetty where the wall crept out.

The wall crept out into the estuary like a thin black finger and there were people standing all along it, some of them with binoculars. Cameras were clicking; the telly man was there; there was a man with a video film whirring.

But I hardly saw them because of the whale. *My* whale. Huge and beautiful like I saw in my dream.

Only, now when I saw it I closed my eyes quick.

Because what had happened to the whale nearly broke my heart.

3
The whale

He was out of the water, though not completely out. He was stuck on a sandbank and you could see his back, smooth and gleaming like a big black mountain. There were two black figures with snorkels on swimming up close and then kicking off, and the figures looked like two tiny tadpoles flapping about my beautiful whale.

And even though there were people about and everyone was looking at the whale, you had the idea of something wild and lonely. Something you could never, ever reach.

Where I was standing there was a lot of noise: people talking to each other and some people laughing. It was Saturday and most of Bigsbury wasn't at work and, anyway, the newspaper and telly men were making more row than anyone. I could hear them talking into microphones with the cameras going in front of them, and what they were saying was sometimes a lie:

'The whale was first spotted at ten o'clock last night by a man out walking his dog. The whale, Moby, is a sperm whale, one of the largest of the whale species. Sperm whales normally inhabit very deep water, living at 1000 feet below the surface. Moby here is in less than ten feet of water. There is concern that the water will not support him and that pressure on his internal organs may eventually cause his death.

'Moby is the first sperm whale to swim down this estuary for over twenty years. At present two divers are engaged in checking Moby to see if he has sustained any serious injuries. It is hoped that Moby may be able to move out into deeper water at high tide this evening. He is believed to be on his way to the Azores, and to have taken a wrong turning.'

One thing for sure is that was a lie: Moby wasn't his name. If he had a name it wouldn't be something ordinary like that. My whale would have a wild, secret name that only other whales could say. I would call him Deep because that's what he was: deep like the sea and deep like a mystery.

I was stood there watching the whale, right? I could see the divers splashing around him and people fussing on the shore. Overhead there was a helicopter droning and someone hanging outside of it. I was watching all that, but I was watching something else as well. Something I didn't know I knew; a secret part of me that was wild like the whale, wanting to leave Bigsbury behind and go off on my own out into the world.

Tears kept coming into my eyes but I didn't feel like crying. I felt like driving all those people away. Chucking their cameras into the water. Tossing their binoculars in and all. If I could have, I would have chucked the *people* in the water, except for the ones who were trying to help.

But I didn't do any of those things. Instead I ran away.

I finished up at Ben's house. Ben's the mate I told you about and he's a wimp like me. Both of us are useless at sports and neither of us much likes joining things. We've even formed the Wimps' Club at school, but the catch is if other kids join (not that anyone wants to), then *we* wouldn't want to belong to it. So, so far there's only the two of us.

When I got to Ben's I rang the bell and he came to the door with a choc-ice in his hand. Without saying anything he left the door open and turned away and I went after him down the hall.

'Bin watching the whale?' he said gloopily. Ice-cream was on the tip of his nose and there was chocolate round his mouth.

'Nah,' I said, telling a lie and shrugging my shoulders dead-casual like. Because it came to me suddenly – *bam*! – that Deep had swum into my head and was waiting there for something. I was feeling him being sad and afraid, and talking about him would be like talking about Dad; it would make me feel disloyal.

'Me neither,' said Ben. 'My mam says it's too cold.' He finished the last bit of choc-ice off and scrunched the paper into a ball. He threw the ball at a basket and missed, then said, 'Listen, Jimbo, I been thinking a bit. We gotta talk about what you should do, because I reckon Barker's got his eye on you.'

'Yeah,' I said. 'Well. So what if he has?' And the way I spoke was grumpy, OK? Because talking made Barker seem that much realer, like he might be after me the way Ben said.

'You want to do something dead quick, me old mate, or he'll do you like he did all the others.'

'Do what?' I asked. And I was getting fed up.

'Hit 'im one before he hits you.'

'Yeah. Right. Me and who else?'

'Well, not me,' Ben said, looking huffed. He took the scarf off that he always wears and then put it back on and tied it again. I had the notion he was enjoying himself. 'It's not me he's after, is it, mate? It's not me he's been and noticed yet. That's why I reckon we gotta talk. See, what you need, Jimbo, is a strategy. Do to him what Mam tells *me* to do. She says bullies back down when you stand up to them, so what I'm saying to you is go and hit 'im first. That'll knock his stuffing out, honest, mate. It'll sort him out good and proper, no sweat, and I'll be right behind you holding your coat.'

'I'll think about it,' I said gloomily.

Ben punched my shoulder and said, 'Do it, mate, before he decides to do *you* instead.'

After Ben said that we mucked about, trying to teach his dog to beg and talking about newts, because that's what Ben likes to talk about, and frogs, but my heart wasn't in it. I kept thinking about Deep, with none of his own kind anywhere near, and maybe dying like that all alone. Then thinking about Deep made me think of Dad.

I got this picture I'd been holding off of Dad on his own in a hospital bed, too ill to walk and too ill to talk, not being able to say what was wrong. Dad was like a giant shadow without a face spreading slowly inside my head, getting trapped there like Deep was trapped in the sand, and I said to Ben, 'I gotta be going.'

Ben looked at me huffily again, 'But you only just *got* here and, besides, you haven't seen my picture of the Great Crested newt.'

I went home anyway. I went the short way round by the Scruff. That's what they call the trees near us, mainly because of the rubbish underneath. If you go far enough in through the trees you can see the estuary, and next to that a manky marina with clapped-out boats and black tarpaulin covering up old fishing gear. Without knowing I was going to do it, I went to the edge of the trees and looked out at the water. On a black day like it was, everything looked black: black water, black chimneys, black gritty beach. Even the hills in the distance turned from purple and yellow to black.

I couldn't see the whale but I could see the road bridge with people on it, like ants peering down for all they were worth, and the helicopter still whirring round. I was stood there waiting for some sign from Deep – just a click in my head would have done it – to show that he knew I was there.

But nothing happened. And suddenly I was freezing cold. My ears were aching and my tummy felt funny. Apart from that it was starting to rain, so I turned myself round and ran through the trees and tried to get home before anyone else.

4
'Everyone knows he's going to die'

The kitchen light was already on and Maddy and Chrissy were both back home.

'Well, a fat lot of good *you* turned out to be!' That was our Chrissy yelling at me, even before I'd took my coat off. 'Pots in the sink! Beds not made! What was it I said you had to do? I said make yourself useful while we've gone! And did you? No! Did you heck!'

When Chrissy said that her face went red the way it does when she's really mad, and all I did was shrug a bit, mainly through not knowing what to say next.

She yelled even louder, 'I expect you went off to look at that whale! That's *exactly* the sort of thing you'd do. No thought in your head for anyone else. And what good will it do the whale, anyhow? Everyone knows he's going to die.'

After Chrissy said that she turned away but I carried on standing where I was. And the funny feeling in my tummy got funnier. It went up gradually from right low down and was suddenly a great thick lump in my mouth.

I was sick all over the kitchen floor and after that I couldn't *stop* being sick. I heard Maddy say, 'The poor pet! You shouldn't go on at him like you do. Hold on a bit, chick, while I fetch a towel.'

A cold wet towel got pressed on my face and a big soft hand started stroking my hair. Then I heard our Chrissy say, 'Well . . . I don't know . . . I didn't think . . . Come here, pet, and let me look at you.'

Being sick's not what I meant to do but it turned out mainly OK in the end, because instead of being moaned at I got put to bed and fussed over. A hot-water bottle went under my feet and a bowl to be sick in was put near my head.

Chrissy said, 'I'm sorry, pet, I didn't mean to go on. But what with Dad and our mam and that . . .' she was near to tears and I was as well, only not (and it shames me to say this now) because of Dad.

You see the weird thing was, I couldn't picture Dad. It's as if the stroke had somehow got between us and instead of seeing him laughing and talking and acting up the way he did, I kept getting this blob like a ghostly shape that cancelled out the Dad I knew.

But I could see Deep all right. It's almost like I had got inside him and felt the fear that he must have felt.

I slept a bit and was sick again for a bit after that. Mam

came in later, in the pitch dark. There was this whiff of bitter orange peel and I could feel her hair tickling my nose. Mam said, 'Poor old duck. Sleep tight, my pet.' Then I heard her tiptoe out the room.

Later I woke up again. You could have heard a pin drop a mile away, and there was no moon showing through the gap in the curtains; all there was was this thick black dark.

I got out of bed and I felt all right. I pulled my clothes on and went down the stairs.

Outside it was even blacker than ever, with just the odd cloud skimming down low, and this smell people call the sea but that's really just seaweed going off. I went down the harbour and no one was there. There was just me and the water and, somewhere, Deep.

I couldn't see him. Not even a shadowy bulk far off. And I couldn't hear him, either. But I knew he was there and away from the sandbank. And this strange idea came into my mind, that Deep's story was our story, Dad's and mine, and neither of us knew what was coming next.

5
Fighting with Deep

Next day Mam made me stay at home. She kept fussing over me and looking upset, like it was her fault I'd somehow got myself ill. The telephone was ringing all day long with people wanting to talk about Dad, and his customers still kept ringing up. Mam said, 'I never knew your dad was thought of so high,' and she looked proud and trembly all at the same time.

At dinner Aunty Mavis came. Aunty Mavis is big and fat. Mam says she's a bonny lass who was always popular with the lads, but that day Aunty Mavis looked glum. Even her lipstick was a dark plum colour and not the usual bright shiny red. And what Aunty did was grab hold of Mam and say, 'I've come to help you out, Milly. You'll need the comfort of family. What a thing to happen, I don't know. You'd think our Ray was much too young.' As if Dad *decided* to have a stroke.

I was on the sofa out of the way, and Aunty came up and

grabbed me and pressed me hard so my nose was in her cushiony chest. A necklace was digging into my face, and there was this pong of perfume that made you cough.

'Jimmy!' she said, pressing hard. 'The littlest one! And so poorly now! What will we do with you? Oh dear me!'

After she said that, she let me go and fumbled in her bag for a handkerchief. Then she coughed and sniffed and dabbed at her eyes, so even though she'd come round to comfort Mam, Mam was the one who comforted *her*. They were cuddling each other and chuntering on, with Aunty Mavis giving great big sighs, when suddenly both of them started to cry – not softly, either, but with ear-splitting yells – and get this, will you, they didn't just cry over Dad like you'd think, they cried over having to queue at Tesco's, and over them stopping the 9.30 train, and their not being able to get pink elastic, and over Uncle Donald's athlete's foot.

In the middle of the crying the telephone rang and Mam said, 'Drat and double drat!' and Aunty Mavis put a hand to her throat. Dad's voice came into the room again, booming out dead loud and clear, then one of his customers coughed and spoke:

'Mrs Wilson? Mrs Roper here. I'm sorry to hear about poor Raymond, but tell him, will you, the job stays his. Oh – and will you tell him Peter's passed his exams, and Uncle Roly's better now. Oh – and the floor looks a treat after last week's blitz.'

That set them both off crying again, but afterwards there was roast pork to eat, except for me (I had scrambled eggs), and the girls who had gone out with their mates. After *that* Mam said, 'We're going round to see Dad now, pet. Stay in the house and keep yourself warm.'

When they'd gone the house was quiet again and you could tell it was Sunday, mostly because there were kids about biking up and down outside or leaning against lamp-posts, looking bored. I flipped on the radio to get the news and got the end of *The Archers* instead, and then some news about Northern Ireland, and then the real news about the whale:

'Moby the sperm whale, who took a wrong turning, last night was freed by the tide from the sandbank where he had been stranded for several hours. It is hoped he will be guided back to the open sea by boats using water canons and sonar equipment.

'Further reports say that three other whales have been spotted at the mouth of the estuary. These whales appear to be waiting for Moby and may be instrumental in him returning to the sea.'

As soon as I heard that I got off the sofa. My anorak was on the peg in the hall and my boots were underneath it, still claggy with mud from yesterday. I put them on, and I knew even then that I meant all the time to go and see Deep.

When I got outside there was a rough old wind, but a

watery sun was trying to get through, and across the estuary you could see some houses, strung out like tiny bone-white flags. When the sun went in they disappeared and the far shore looked black and empty again.

At the quayside it was like some kind of fair. People were selling hot-dogs and ice-cream, the chip shop was open with a great long queue, and the cameras and microphones were out.

I elbowed my way to the front of the crush and straight in front of me was Deep.

Deep was rising up like a massive island and spraying water off the top of his head. Each time he sprayed the watchers went, 'Aah!' and the people who were standing up on the bridge leant further over and began to cheer.

But I didn't feel like cheering. There was an ache in my heart as if the cameras and the people looking and pointing had put a hole in it. Under my breath I heard myself mutter, 'Deep, Deep. Come on, Deep, you can make it. Honest you can.' If I could have swum out to him I would have done, but instead of swimming I closed myself off, so I wasn't just standing there looking on, but I *was* Deep. I don't mean his poor body that was all you could see, but his wild brain and his wild breath struggling out there in the mucky waves.

Deep. You can make it. Come on, Deep.

In my own head there was this film of dark, like a cloth had come down over it, and in the dark I was fighting hard; I was on my own and I was struggling like mad to try and understand where I was. And I was fetching back a memory, right? Of distant water, icy and blue and crystal clear. Other whales were in the water and they were pushing against me and chattering. What I could hear was *click, click-click,* like someone laughing in your ear.

I *was* Deep, but I was me as well, fighting with him and being a whale, and maybe fighting for myself, too, trying to see Dad the way he really was, and not the way Mam had described him.

But I couldn't keep it up. When the cloth lifted there was this burst of light like an arrow pointing at my head, and another cheer from the watchers went up.

I saw Deep sink very slowly, with amazing grace, back into the filthy, slopping waves, and a line of boats strung out on the water started spraying him even more fiercely and banging about and making a din.

'It's to try and create a wall of noise.' (A bloke said that, right near my ear.) 'It's to make him turn round and go back to sea, but I don't reckon he'll make it now. He's daft, if you ask me. He doesn't know what's good for him.'

The bloke he was talking to laughed out loud, and I wondered what it would feel like to think that was funny.

After Deep vanished I moved off again, but instead of taking myself back home I went down the road into Cairngorm Close.

Cairngorm Close is the posh part of town. It's got brand-new houses with balconies and little trees planted in skinny rows, and a sign put up that says RESIDENTS ONLY in big black letters high up on a pole.

I ignored the sign and went through an archway and on to some grass with the stick-like trees. From Cairngorm Close you can see the estuary spread out in front like a long black scarf. When the sun comes out the scarf turns to grey with flecks of green and little white bits, like it's made out of some kind of watery tweed.

I was scanning the estuary for signs of Deep, wanting him to see me on my own so he'd know right away I was on his side. I looked and looked until my eyes went watery with looking. But he didn't come up. I couldn't even see a shadow of him looming about under the waves. In the end I was having a last long stare when a window went up behind where I was and this voice shouted out, 'Boy! Boy! What are you doing? Have you business in the close or are you a trespasser off the estate?'

A lady with hair like a tight grey hat was shouting at me fit to bust, so I pulled up the hood on my anorak and went back through the archway into the street and under the subway.

The others arrived home just after me. By then I was back on the sofa with a blanket pulled up, and I was shivering a bit because I'd got so cold and I expect the wind had made my face go pale.

Mam came up to me straight away and said, 'Jimmy, my pet, are you all right? You're looking peaky. Let's feel your head. Now, do you want to lie down or would you like some tea?'

Chrissy gave me a very sharp look and opened her mouth and closed it again. Then Aunty came over and said, 'Poor little lamb! Fancy us leaving him all on his own, and him so poorly-looking and all.'

I thought she was going to hug me again, so I gave this sneeze and she shot away, and Madeline said, 'Are you all right, pet? You look a bit poorly still to me.'

Then Chrissy came up and hissed in my ear, 'You've been up to something! You can't fool me – I know that look – you've been up to no good!'

In the end though, everything settled down and I ate some peaches with evaporated milk, and Mam came up and sat next to me. 'Your dad's a bit livelier now, Jimmy – or, at least, he's managing to half sit up. I took him some grapes and a box of figs – not fresh, mind. Dried. Best Maroc. And a mango that's maybe a mite overripe.'

While Mam was speaking she stroked my hair, then said very softly, 'You can go tomorrow. I asked the nurse. She said he'll be perking up and he'll want to see you. Only listen, Jimmy, your dad can't speak. It seems like that bit of his brain's not doing too well, but it might get better. It's early days yet.'

Later she put this record on, and it was one of Dad's favourites that we all hate. Dad used to sing it into an imaginary mike. He'd do the gestures and spin the mike and have this stupid smile on his face. Now the music came into the room and instead of being awful it was sad. *'I did it my way . . .'* came floating out and suddenly I could see Dad's face dead clear, with the soupy smile in place.

I started to laugh and Maddy looked at me and put a finger over her lips. But I couldn't stop and then Mam laughed as well and started to mouth the stupid words. All at once we were *all* singing! Bellowing out at the top of our voices, and even Aunty Mavis joined in.

By the time we all finished it was later still. Aunty Mavis got up and put on her coat. Then she came over to the sofa where I was lying and pinched my chin and slipped a pound in my hand.

'Well *honestly*!' Chrissy said, when she'd gone. 'Talk about the wages of sin.'

I didn't know what she meant by that and, anyway, I was suddenly tired.

Madeline kept saying, 'Poor little Jimmy,' and looking at me with big damp eyes.

And Chrissy was chuntering on all the time, 'You always fall on your feet, our Jimmy. I don't know what Aunty sees in you.'

I'd had enough of both of the girls; they're too big and

busty and they talk too much. So I went to bed and lay there for a bit, just staring into the pitch-black room and thinking about Deep and what he'd do. Willing like mad for him to escape.

After that our dad came into my mind – and you know something? I was suddenly scared. He was my dad and I was scared to see him even though I wanted to. But I wasn't scared like when Barker acts up. This was a different sort of scared, more like I'd never feel safe again.

And that was stupid because I was in my bed, safe and sound with the doors locked up and Mam and the girls dead close at hand.

Only, if I let it happen it came again. This hole like I got when I looked at Deep. And I kept wondering if it would go away or get worse tomorrow when I went to see Dad.

6
Bashing Barker

But before there was Dad there was Barker.

As soon as I got to the playground on Monday he was there, large as life and twice as ugly. He was standing with some other kids and even though he wasn't doing anything, he looked mean enough to make you *think* he would if you were daft enough to get in his way.

Ben was with me and he'd got a cold. He kept sneezing and coughing and then wiping his nose on the tail-end of his scarf. Ben said, 'Mam says I shouldn't be at school. She says I'm delicate, what with me chest. Only I reckoned I'd better come, Jimbo, just to show I'm on your side.' When he said that he gave me a nudge, so his bony elbow went in my ribs. 'You remember, what we said about bashing Barker – and what my mam said about standing up for yourself? So, go on then – go up and hit 'im like we said – and listen, mate, I'll be with you, right?'

Up until then Barker hadn't even noticed me and maybe he wouldn't have, I don't know. But what Ben said set me off all at once thinking things I was trying *not* to think: about Dad not speaking at all or larking about like he used to do, but just lying where he was in his hospital bed; about the man who laughed at Deep.

And there was Ben behind me going, 'Do 'im, mate! Go on – hit 'im like we said!'

And Barker with his thumbs in the belt of his jeans, not taking any notice of us but making me mad just by *being* there.

After that Barker and the man who laughed seemed to run together in a big red blur. And the laugh got louder and louder: *haar*! *Haar*! *HAAR*! All mixed in with Dad and Deep.

Next thing is, I'm up behind Barker and pulling away at his stupid sleeve. Then this weedy voice comes out of my mouth: 'Right then, Barker, I'm going to do you!'

Up went my fist and that's as far as I got, because right after that *his* fist came out and he bashed me – *wham*! – across my nose. That's when I'm sprawled and seeing stars and I heard Miss Gray saying, 'Not you again!'

Then the other kids started telling her things like: '*He* was the one who started it, Miss!' and 'Barker was stood there minding his own and Jimmy Wilson came up and tried to belt 'im one!'

I got to my feet all wobbly and faint, with blood running

down from a cut on my nose – and guess what, will you? There was no sign of Ben. Well, although he's my mate, he's a wimp like me.

So, anyway, Miss Gray shakes her head and takes my arm, and I get marched off to the Head's office, and I've already got this red card, right? And now I'm in trouble for hitting Barker, and Mrs Kershaw says, 'JIMMY WILSON! TROUBLE MAKER! WHAT HAVE YOU GOT TO SAY TO ME?'

She fixed me with this hard, fierce look and then I saw her suddenly think something. Before I could answer she came round her desk and put a hand on top of my head. Her hand was big and soft and plump, not like my mam's that's thin and rough. The Head said: 'Things aren't too good for you now, Jimmy. I understand that it's hard at home; you'll be missing your father, of course you will. But you can talk to me or Miss Gray any time. Only listen, Jimmy, because this is important: if things are bad you have to try harder, for your mum and dad's sake as well as your own. And that means keeping *away* from trouble. So will you do that, Jimmy? Will you have a try?'

I nodded my head and gave this sniff, and the Head said, 'For goodness sake, Jimmy! Here, take this and wipe your nose. And you'd better wash that blood off your face before you go back to Miss Gray's classroom.'

She gave me a tissue and then turned away so I knew I had to leave the room, and I never even got to say anything, like: it wasn't *me* going looking for trouble. Like: it just kind of happened and I don't know how.

The morning passed fast, and at dinner-time I went to the school library. I found a book about whales on the shelf, and there's a picture of a whale in colour on the front. The whale in the picture's not like Deep because he has this fin on top of his back, but he has the same wild, lonely look, as if he's been where he is for ever and ever, and he'll carry on being there after we've all gone.

I read about sperm whales while I ate my snap (two cheese sandwiches and a bunch of black grapes) and the book said that whales have skin like gold leaf; that thin and fine you could peel it off and see through it if you wanted to. Delicate. Easily damaged if they're not in clean sea. And they live in groups and have families; they look after each other all the time and they don't abandon other whales that are sick.

After I read that I couldn't finish my sandwich. I was looking inside myself and finding Deep there like you do in a dream, only more clear and brighter than that. I was seeing Deep and I was seeing other whales as well, waiting for him out in the cold North Sea. In my head I could hear them chattering, *click, click, clickety-click,* only not chattering like they were before, kind of laughing and happy because they were free. This chatter was sharp and fast. It sounded more like Morse code, and I knew they were worried because of Deep.

If I could have done, I'd have skived off school and gone on the bridge for a better view. I would have willed Deep to turn himself round, to swim for the open sea again, to head for his family that were waiting for him. It was what I wanted more than pleasing the Head or bashing Barker. Because I knew, clear as daylight, that if Deep didn't manage to get back to the sea, then nothing would go right, ever again.

7
'Your dad's still your dad'

Mam met me from school with her coat flying open and her overall still on underneath it. You could see where she'd been lugging spuds around from the brown mark down her front. When Mam saw me she gave me a hug and said, 'Come on, pet, we'll go and see your dad. The girls won't be visiting until later on, so you can have him all to yourself for a while.'

'You been to work?' I asked, surprised. And somehow it managed to come out wrong, like I was blaming her for something.

'We have to have money coming in,' she said, 'and with your dad laid up for I-don't-know-how-long . . . that's how things are. I've asked Mr Baverstock if I can do extra hours.'

'But what about Dad? He'll be on his own. He won't have anybody there he knows.'

'I know that, pet, but it can't be helped. I'll go and see him when I can.'

'But . . .' I began, when Mam said, 'Jimmy!' and that's all she said, but what it meant was, don't you go talking on like that. So I shut my mouth and kept it shut, because somehow I seemed to have got the day wrong. It's like this big black cloud had come down *plop* and swallowed all my good intentions up.

We went through the town to the hospital and Mam was talking all the time, saying, 'That Mr Baverstock, talk about mean! He takes all the old, droopy lettuce leaves off and then puts up the price when he sells the heart. Heart! *He* hasn't got one if you were to ask me.'

When we reached the hospital it was getting dark. You could see big square windows all lit up and people inside like black shadows moving. And I could feel my heart going *bump, bump, bump,* as if it knew something I didn't know yet. There were cars going in and out all the time, and an ambulance, and a taxi waiting.

Inside the hospital there was this pong of dead dinners and disinfectant like you get in the toilets at school. It's the sort of pong that makes your toes curl up, but Mam didn't seem to notice. She went marching on with me trailing after, and I could feel my feet getting slower and slower. I had this idea that the day had stolen something else off me, so my bottle wasn't there when I wanted it.

When we got to the ward there were two swing doors with a notice over saying ST OKE UNIT in big black letters with the 'R' disappeared. I stopped again and stayed where I was, and Mam said, 'Jimmy!' impatiently, this time meaning, come on, will you? Don't hang about. We haven't got all day.

Mam pushed at the door and then turned back to me. She stopped her bustling all at once and and took my face in her two hard hands. Very softly she said, 'Your dad's still your dad. Don't let him see how upset you are,' and then she pinched my cheek and pushed the door open and we both went through.

That's when this nurse came sailing up. She said, 'Mrs Wilson! Is this your Jimmy? What a fine young lad he is, to be sure!' And *she* took my face and gave it a pinch so it was fairly tingling and red by then. After that the nurse goes, 'Don't worry, pet, it's early days yet. Just give your dad a nice big smile.'

When we got to Dad he was on this bed, and when he saw me come in he didn't move. Not his arms, not his legs, not even his face. Dad's face looked like a plastic mask, dead white like that, and still. You had the notion that although his eyes were pointed at us, it wasn't us he was really seeing. It was more like he was looking at *himself*. More like a light had got switched off and he was on his own in the dark.

'Ray! Here's our Jimmy come to give you a hug.' Mam nodded at me and gave me a smile and the smile said, just as if she'd spoken, go on then, Jimmy. Do it, or else!

I wanted to go but my feet felt heavy. They took me up to

the side of the bed but when I got there I couldn't do what Mam said. I could hear her behind me going, 'Come on, our Jim.'

Only, Dad was angry. I could tell right off. And maybe he was angry with me. It's like he'd found this place inside himself that made him angry with everyone, and that was the place he wanted to stay.

In the end I plonked a kiss on his cheek and then backed away from the bed dead fast. And Mam said cheerily, 'That's right, love,' while she came up to Dad and kissed him herself and said, 'I've brought you some plums, Ray. Not Victoria, but sweet enough. And Baverstock's sent you these chrysanths.'

Mam dived in the bag she always carries and pulled out a bunch of shaggy flowers with their petals curling and going brown at the tips. 'Tsch! Tsch! Isn't that just Baverstock all over? Too flaming mean to give owt for nowt. Well! This is what I think of them!'

She dumped the flowers into the bin and took the plums out of her bag, then sat there looking flummoxed for once. Because every inch of space round our dad's bed already had fruit on it. There was even a marrow leant against his bed-leg and tomatoes were sprouting round his headphones.

Mam wedged the bag of plums near Dad's arm. Then she kissed him again and said, 'I'll leave you with Jim – I reckon he could help you out with those grapes, and I'll come in later and peel you an orange. You've got to keep your strength up, pet. Maybe you could manage a banana for tea?'

She got up to go and said to me, 'Talk to him, love. He'd like that, you know. Tell him what you've been doing at school.' Then she upped and left me on my own.

8
Dad and me

To begin with I held back a bit, amazed by what I had to do, because I wasn't that used to talking to Dad.

You see, I never usually managed to get him on his own. When he was at home and things were OK there was Madeline and Chrissy and Mam as well, all of them fussing about over him and Dad mostly enjoying the fuss. If I *did* manage to say something out loud, one of the girls would jump in quick. They'd go, 'Take no notice! Jimmy makes stuff up. He's a story-teller is Jimmy Wilson. You can't believe a thing he says.'

Then Dad would laugh and punch my chest and say, 'There's nothing wrong with a bit of old blarney. It's the Irish in him coming out.'

Why did everyone always laugh and no one ever believe what I said? Even Mam when she was being kind said, 'I don't know what to make of you, Jim. The stories you tell! I don't know where you get them from!'

And that would make Dad laugh again, because Dad's a person who likes to laugh. If something goes wrong he doesn't get cross, he gives this shrug and spreads his hands and makes a joke.

That's what he did when Joey died (Joey's the budgie I told you about). He was blue and could talk if he wanted to. He'd say, 'Time for bed, Joey. Time for bed,' and the day he died we'd got this box. The box was all lined with cotton wool, and we'd dug a hole in the garden for him and were going to put him in it real neat, with a rose bush planted on the top.

Then Dad came over and picked Joey up and plonked him *plop* on the cotton wool, and said, 'Time for bed, Joey! Time for bed!'

He couldn't help laughing, even when things were really bad, like when his sandwich business went bust and Mam was panicking and getting upset. Dad put his hands on both her shoulders and laughed at her and said, 'Don't you worry, pet. I'm not down yet. I'll just go out and earn more bread!'

But now there was only Dad and me. When I turned round from looking out the window, I took the bag of plums off his arm, then pulled up the scruffy plastic chair and sat myself down in front of him.

After that I took a deep breath and said, as loud as anything, 'Right then, Dad. There's this kid at school. Barker's 'is name and he's big as *that*. I'm telling you! He's a real big lad. And the thing is, Dad, I don't like him much. He gets up my nose with the stuff he does, so today I go up and tell him so, and then he gets mad and I clock 'im one, right? Smack on top of his stupid big nose.

'Well, down he goes *splat* on to the ground, though not before he's had a go at me. He gets one in, but it doesn't hurt much and then – *wham*! He's down on the ground, like I said, and I'm stood there looking while the other kids cheer. But me – I just shrug and stroll off like that, all nonchalant, like, because that's how I am. And you know something else, Dad?'

I leant in closer when I said that and looked at Dad's face, at his angry eyes. And I daresay I should have given up then, but I didn't. It's like I wanted to give up saying what I was but I wanted something else as well. Maybe for Dad to stop looking angry. Or maybe for him to believe me for once.

I carried on. 'If Barker starts acting up again, I'll clock 'im another across his chops. *That'll* teach him to mix it with me, because Barker's sort always back down in the end.'

When I finished speaking I stayed in my chair and folded my arms across my chest. And perhaps I expected something to happen. Like Dad to jump up and call me a liar, or our Chrissy to suddenly pop up and say, 'You're a fibber, our Jimmy! You know you are!' But nothing happened. And you know something? I felt dead happy then. Even with Dad the way he was, and even knowing I'd told him a lie. I liked this new kid that I'd made. I liked him better than Jimmy Wilson. And it came to me in another flash that I might get to *be* the hero for once.

So I sat where I was and ate some grapes and just stayed there quiet until Mam came back. She came bustling in all bright and breezy, as if the way Dad used to be had rubbed off on her.

'There you are are, my pet!' she said straight away, like she didn't expect to see me at all. 'I can tell you've been talking your dad to death! Well! I don't know – you men! You're worse than the ladies when you get together. Now, Ray, will you have that banana? I've peeled it, look! Will you have a bite of it just for me?'

Mam pushed the banana towards Dad's mouth, and he turned his face away from her and kept it turned to the tall black window. In the window you could see Dad's double, only long and weird-looking and scary, as if he had turned into his own dark ghost.

Mam put the banana on top of the grapes and bent down to Dad and kissed his head, 'I'll see you tomorrow, my pet,' she said. 'I'll bring you some figs, they'll cheer you up! Tunisian. Plump. Just come in. Tarra, then, ducky, don't look so glum – and don't do anything I wouldn't do!'

We went out of the alcove where Dad was and into the corridor off the ward. And Mam was walking fast, like that.

You could hear her feet going *clonk, clonk, clonk* and her bag was thumping against her side. We went past a stall selling newspapers and a stand with different leaflets on. We were nearly at the big swing doors, when all at once I stood stock-still. Mam was with me, holding my arm, and when I stopped, she stopped – *bam*! – and her shoes made a squeaking noise on the floor.

She said, 'What's the matter, Jimmy? Are you feeling sick?'

'You've got to stop talking fruit,' I said.

'Eh? What are you on about, Jimmy, love? Is this another of your funny ideas?'

'You've got to stop talking fruit to Dad.'

'But, Jimmy, love,' Mam put her bag down on the floor as if it suddenly weighed too much, 'fruit's what I *do*. I know about fruit. And working for Baverstock – it's how I spend my days.'

'Yeah, well.' I shrugged my shoulders and picked up a leaflet all about feet. There was a picture of a giant toe on the front and a heading said: *Bunions! Veroukas! Athlete's Foot!* 'Maybe you should talk about something else.'

Mam stood there looking flummoxed again. I could tell she thought I might say something else, but I didn't. I picked up her bag and started walking with it towards the door. Then her feet came clonking after me. When we got to the door it was raining hard and Mam said, 'You're a rare one,

Jimmy, I can tell you that! You and the funny ideas you get! Come on, pet, we'd best make a run for it. I've some mushrooms in the bag for tea.'

We got home wet and the radio was on and Madeline was fussing about at the stove. She said, 'Make yourself useful, Jimmy, for once, and set the table while I make some toast.'

She put some knives and forks in my hand at the same time as the news came on. I plonked them down on the tablecloth and cocked an ear to the radio. At first there was nothing much to hear, just boring stuff about banks and that. And then the newsreader's voice seemed to change.

I was stood there, right, and I'd a plate in my hand. I was listening to the news like that, with Madeline and Chrissy chuntering on, and this newsreader said:

'Moby, the sperm whale who was washed down the estuary last week, is stranded on a sandbank again. In spite of efforts to head him off, Moby went back under the bridges today and was stranded at low tide.

'It is now believed that Moby may have drifted into the estuary because he was out of condition due to lack of suitable food in the North Sea. If that is so, then the outlook for him is bleak. Large whales such as Moby do not normally survive for long periods in shallow water, and without access to their usual diet of giant squid.

'Now for a recap of todays other news . . .'

There's this sound that shock makes inside your head, like

a giant wave crashing. After I heard the news about Deep, the wave in my head got louder and bigger. Then there was the sound of a crash and a bang. The plate I was holding went on the floor and Chrissy said, 'Well, *honestly*, Jimmy. That's the only thing you had to do and you had to go and do it wrong.'

And Madeline said, 'It's that whale again, getting to you, isn't it, Jimmy? You mustn't go upsetting yourself. It's only an animal, when all's said and done.'

What she meant to say was, have you forgotten Dad? He's more important than a whale.

Only somehow that didn't help at all. Because to me, Deep was more than just a whale. He *was* me, and he was Dad as well. He was everything that we wanted to be or could be if we got some luck. And now he was trapped and maybe he was dying, and the wave in my head got louder again.

I sat on my chair when we had our tea, but I couldn't manage to get anything down. And Mam said kindly, 'Are you poorly again? Or have you just eaten something you shouldn't?'

After tea I went straight up to bed and stayed there until the house settled down. I heard Madeline come up, and Chrissy giggle, and then Mam shooting the bolt in the door. Madeline came in and kissed the top of my head, 'Nightie-night, our Jimmy. Sleep tight.'

After that it went dead quiet again and I got out of bed and dressed myself. Then I crept out the house as quiet as I could and shut the door so the latch stayed up. I walked down the road in the hissing rain – and then suddenly I started to run, under the subway with its manky white tiles, through the town with its closed-up shops, down to the estuary and Deep.

There was no sign of Deep. No one else was out that night and to begin with I just stood there, watching the waves and listening to the sloppy noise they made. Rain was hammering on to the hood of my anorak and it sounded like bullets going *pop-pop-pop*.

But I could feel Deep like a friend, being there. I felt closer to him than to Dad, even, or to Mam and the girls. Except that this closeness was a lonely thing. I could feel Deep knowing all the unsaid things that were floating around in my skull.

Dad might die. That was one of the things.

Or he might not be able to speak again.

He might not be able to work or laugh or do the things he liked to do.

Dad might stay angry and silent and Mam might stay at Baverstock's, forever lugging spuds about.

I hunched my shoulders against the rain at the same time as I heard a noise, a kind of slow *put-put*. Then I saw a boat just under the bridge and another boat behind it. They hovered together before the motors went dead, and after that the dark swirled in. All I could see was the dark and the rain and a lamp in a window beind the quay. I was getting cold right through to my chest, so I turned and ran for it towards the road bridge.

When you're on that bridge you can feel it move. The thrum of the traffic goes through your feet, and the wind's like you might think a hurricane is: *bzooom*! *Bzooom*! *Bzooom*! You've to hang like death to the metal bars or it knocks you down and you can't get up. And you're not supposed to *be* on the bridge.

But I knew that Deep was underneath it.

Then all at once I got a glimpse of him. His back was like a warship out of the waves, and even while I was watching and clinging to the rails, a great wave came up and sucked him in.

The way he went, softly, slowly, gently, like that, without a sound and without any fuss, made my insides squeeze together. It's like I was calm the way Deep was, but shaken and upset as well.

Deep went down and he didn't come up. I wanted him to move towards the sea, but after he sank it was as black as pitch.

I got back home and let myself in. I was shivering and I couldn't keep still, but I got into bed and went to sleep.

9
'Jimmy Wilson is a wimp'

The morning after, I was eating cereal and my eyes were watering and red. I felt rough like the estuary is in the wind, and wanting to cough but not doing it in case Mam noticed and kept me in. So I ate this cereal with the girls there chuntering away to each other and sometimes shouting across at me:

'Jimmy! You haven't washed your neck.'

'Eat with your mouth shut, for goodness' sake.'

'What happened to your gloves – have you lost them again?'

Stuff like that as gets on your nerves. I was trying not to cough or lip back at the girls, and Mam was busy making a list of stuff she'd got to do that day:

'Go to Baverstock's. Work till twelve.

'Remember to pick up some bread on the way.

'Iron Ray's pyjamas. Visit him. Ring up this morning before you go out.'

All in all there was a lot of noise, the way there is in our house every day.

Then the news came on: this geezer with the jolly voice, making out that Deep was a joke for when the real news was done.

'Moby the whale was released last night from the sandbank where he had been beached again. Police in launches watched him through night binoculars until shortly before midnight when the high tide swept him off the bank.

'A flotilla of boats have been revving their engines behind him this morning, trying to create a wall of sound in the hope that Moby will head away from them and join his friends in the open sea. Traffic on the road bridge has been slowed down deliberately so that the noise will not panic Moby and make him head back up the estuary.'

I put my spoon down and thought about skiving off school again. It came to me that if I was with Deep, if I was where I could see him even if he couldn't see me, he would know about me somehow and he'd go the right way.

But Chrissy's so sharp she'll cut herself. She looked over at me and said, 'I'll be going your way this morning, our Jim. I'll make sure and go with you to school.'

'What a good girl you are, Chrissy,' said Mam. 'Real thoughtful if you were to ask me – and you're a lucky lad, Jimmy Wilson, to have a sister as good as our Chris.'

So I went to school. And trouble waited until I was

feeling safe. Barker was in the yard again and he wasn't even looking my way. He was scuffling over something with one of his mates, and Ben was there, only not with Barker, but kind of hanging back and watching him. He was wearing a red scarf his mam had knitted with bobbles on the ends.

When I saw Ben he wiped his nose on one of the bobbles and then sidled up. 'I gotta look like I'm not with you,' he hissed. 'See, I don't want Barker to notice me – only, watch it, mate, he ain't done yet.'

After that we went in to school. We did our sums to get settled down, and then wrote a story about a witch, and then we all went into the hall.

It was Assembly, the way it is every morning, and all the school was sitting in rows. Wendy Gibson was monitor, sitting on a special chair at the front and looking mighty pleased with herself. She had to jump up quick when she got a sign and switch the projector on at the right time, so the words of the songs came up on the wall.

We were all singing and clapping, the usual stuff. We'd sung:

Give your right hand to Jesus
Give your left hand to me
Let's make a circle
For the whole world to see . . .

On and on like that, with Mrs Kershaw counting the beat and making us stop because we were singing too loud or in the wrong places or we weren't singing loud enough. Then she gave us a talk about being polite and noticing things we hadn't noticed before. She told us there were posters being put on the walls that said:

Predict!
Observe!
Think what is happening!
Why?

When she finished nattering we had to learn a new song. And to begin with that was the same as usual. Mrs Kershaw said the first two lines:

I love Jesus
And he loves me!

And we shouted it after her and clapped too loud or not loud enough, and Mrs Kershaw said what she usually said: 'Andrew Barker, I'm looking at you! I looked at you yesterday! Don't let me have to look at you again!' Then she gave Wendy Gibson a wave with her hand and Wendy jumped up smartish and flicked the projector for the words of the song to come up in red ink. And that's when everything went wrong.

Because instead of it saying the words of the song, it said: JIMMY WILSON IS A WIMP!!! in big red letters.

Some of the kids already had their mouths open to sing the new song, and they closed them again quick, and just for a moment, nothing happened. Mrs Kershaw was getting ready to conduct the singing, not knowing what was written on the wall behind. Then suddenly everyone started to laugh. I was getting looked at and pointed at, and my ears and my nose were going bright red. Then Mrs Kershaw looked behind her and gave a jump and banged down her ruler and said, 'BE QUIET ALL OF YOU. AT ONCE! I SHALL BE FINDING OUT WHO DID THIS!' Then: 'Jimmy Wilson! In my office after Assembly. Immediately, if you please!'

And none of it was even my fault!

I went to see Mrs Kershaw again, who looked at me and shook her head, and I told her I didn't know who did it, because you don't go grassing someone up, even Barker who I hate. So I told this lie and went back to 5b and Carol Spragg came up at break and tried to put her arm through mine. She said, 'Well, I don't mind you being a wimp. I don't like rough boys. I like you.' And that didn't make things any better, as a matter of fact it made them *worse*, so I was glad in a way when school was over and Mam was waiting for me again.

But I could tell straight away that something was up.

10
'Wake up, Deep!'

Mam's skin looked frozen, a kind of stiff, dead-white, like all her blood had run away and left an empty face behind.

'Ducky – your dad won't see us today.' Mam gabbled the words real fast like that, as if saying them quick might make them less true or I might not notice what she'd really said.

'Why not?' I said, and sniffed with cold, and Mam gave me a hanky out of her pocket, smelling of apples and peppermint. Then she put her arm round my shoulders and we walked along with the cold wind in our faces and rain beginning to spatter down.

When we'd gone down the street a little way Mam stood stock-still, smack in the middle of the busy pavement. She said, 'I went at dinner and your dad was there. He didn't speak. He never does. The nurses say he probably could, and that maybe he's *deliberately* quiet. They say he's mad because of what happened. Can't sort it out and accept it, like – but,

Jimmy! He looked that mad at *me*! He tried to chuck an apple at me, and the nurse said I'd better leave it for then.'

Mam's eyes were running, maybe with the cold.

After a while I said, 'I've got a story I wrote at school. I'll show it to you, if you like.'

And Mam hugged me and got out another hanky and wiped her runny eyes with it. She said, 'Ah, Jimmy! What would I do without you, pet?' Then we began to walk slowly on again.

At tea Mam told the girls what had happened with Dad. 'The nurse said had we got a dog? And I said no we hadn't, why? And *she* said, well, they'll often speak to a dog. She said animals seemed to soothe people down and make them more accepting, like, so they don't mind being ill so much.'

'There's next door's cat,' our Madeline said. 'He'd love that, Mam! That'd make him speak! D'you remember when it got that pigeon and wouldn't give it up to him? He was shouting at it, and cussing as well. And *Mrs* Pidgeon came outside and said, "Cocoa! Take no notice of that naughty man. Come inside to the conservatory and sit on Mummy's knee." '

We had a good laugh when we remembered that and it made Dad more like himself again.

Later we had the telly on while the girls did their homework upstairs in their room. Mam sat in her chair with her feet tucked up. She didn't say very much that night and you could tell she wasn't taking anything in but instead was thinking really hard, dark stuff she daren't say out loud.

Later still I went outside.

I didn't mean to go back to the estuary but I got drawn there. The harbour wall was covered with frost that glittered in the pale moonlight. I was looking at the wall with the water behind it, flat and shivery under the moon, when a man nearby said, 'Oy! You there! You looking for Moby are you, son? He's disappeared. There's been no sign all day. The boats that were trying to head him out have gone off to do some other work. And nobody's seen him out at sea.'

When the man said that he turned away and I carried on walking round the harbour wall to where the end of it dropped down to the estuary. There was nobody around and no sound, even of water lapping. It seemed to me then that I was on my own, properly, for the very first time, and the whole night was somehow holding its breath. Or as if I'd dreamt Deep up the way I thought I had at the start.

'Deep,' I said, very softly, more like I was talking to myself than really calling Deep.

And he was there straight away, I swear to you. He was in my head, almost at once. But he wasn't chattering or moving about or getting upset at the traffic noise.

Deep was dreamy and lost in himself. He wasn't seeing the clear blue sea or listening to his mates calling; he was drifting slowly off to sleep, very calmly and deliberately. I could feel the darkness creeping up and the water rocking like a black cradle. Then the darkness creeping again.

'Deep!' I shouted. 'Wake up, Deep! Don't go to sleep! If you go to sleep you'll never wake up! Deep! Deep! Wake up now!'

But nothing happened. Just a cormorant out too late rushed up in front of me and flew away.

And after that *I* ran away. I was too scared and too full of sadness to stay with Deep. Only I didn't run home to Mam and the girls, I went to the hospital.

11
Waking Dad

It was only seven o'clock but it seemed late, and the lights inside seemed too bright and too white. There was me skidding down the corridor, leaving all that dark behind, and screeching through the double doors at the entrance to Dad's ward. A nurse came over. She peered behind me with her eyebrows up and said, 'It's Jimmy, love, isn't it? Are you on your own? Or is one of the girls waiting for you outside? Your dad's not been any too well, I'm afraid. Nothing to worry yourself about – but perhaps you should come again tomorrow, when he's feeling more the thing?'

We were standing next to this great big board with a picture of a man drawn on it. Bits of the man had labels on saying: *Loss of Feeling. Anxiety.* Then, right at the bottom: *Poor Bladder Control.*

I shrugged the nurse off without meaning to and stamped off to where Dad had his bed. I pulled up a chair with some squashed grapes on and sat myself down and stared at him.

And straight away I could see that Dad was still angry. When I came up to the bed he didn't move or even look at me properly; his eyes went flicking left and right and then they flicked on to the window and stayed there as if I hadn't come in. It made me forget that Dad was ill and think that he was just being stupid because that was how he wanted to be.

So I pulled my chair up even closer and grabbed hold of his slack, dead arm and pulled it hard and kept on pulling. Then I yelled, 'Dad! Dad! I know you're not deaf! Will you stop doing that and look at me! I've something I want to say to you and you're not even listening, and I've run all this way!'

My voice went funny like it goes when you've got a frog in your throat. My nose was running and I got out Mam's hanky and wiped it and had a good long cough. Then I said to Dad, who was still not looking but pretending he hadn't even heard what I said, 'I had another go at Barker, today. Talk about laugh! I didn't smash him, though, I had a better idea than that. What I did was write this thing on some paper that should have had a song on it. And the paper got projected up on the wall in the middle of Assembly. And d'you know what I put on the paper, Dad? You'll laugh at this, I put: ANDREW BARKER IS A WIMP! so everyone in the school saw it, and everyone laughed dead hard at him, and Mrs Kershaw told him she wanted to see him as soon as we'd finished in the hall.'

After I said that I leant back a bit and I thought Dad was going to stay how he was. But he didn't. He started to turn his head, very slowly and carefully, until it had swivelled round towards my face and we were looking at each other, eye to eye, with me not knowing what else to say.

And that's when I thought I saw something, like a spark flashing or a gleam in his eye. It was there and it was gone like *that*. He suddenly looked like my dad again.

So I sat some more and told him stuff about school and that. But I never went and mentioned Deep. Keeping Deep a secret meant keeping him safe. Deep was our luck, right? A kind of miracle that had come our way. That's why he had to have luck of his own.

I nattered on to Dad for a while, and then I saw his head go down on his chest. A nurse appeared and touched my shoulder. 'He's tired now, precious, you run off home. Come back tomorrow and see him again.'

I went out the ward and got off home, and Chrissy was there saying, 'Where have you been? You've been out, haven't you? To look at that whale. Why don't you leave the poor thing alone? Get your coat off before Mam sees you. She's that exhausted she's fallen asleep – *and*, Jimmy Wilson, that's as well for you!'

Maddy gave me a small, quick smile and said very softly,

'There's some toffees for you in the drawer in my room.'

I took my coat off and went to sit down, and Chrissy brought me over a mug of hot milk. She rubbed a hand through my cold, damp hair and said, 'I've put a hot-water bottle in your bed. You'd better go off soon and get warmed up. There's honey in that milk to help it down. And, Jimmy, mind you have a proper wash, right? Or you'll be getting warmed up another way!'

Later I was lying in my bed and trying to remember how Dad looked before he went and had his stroke. But the funny thing was I couldn't remember; all I could see was this stiff, white face. The only time I could see our dad was when I was sleeping and having a dream. We were back in his sandwich bar and Dad was larking about with the customers, saying, 'Does cheese and pickle tickle your fancy?' or 'Now, now, Dorothy, you're not egg and cress, you're definitely a chicken with spice. And, Mr Mullhoney, you're beef for sure, with mustard on, if you were to ask me.'

I dreamt like that and then I woke up and couldn't get back to sleep again. I kept thinking about Deep. If Deep went to sleep he would die for sure, and I was scared that's what he was going to do in spite of my being there inside his head.

He might die soon, maybe tomorrow, and there was no way I could save him now. It was up to Deep to decide to live.

12
Deep's decision

I listened to the news while I ate my porridge.

'There is still no sign of Moby, the whale. Police scanned the estuary again last night but Moby didn't surface. Other whales waiting for Moby out in the North Sea have given up their vigil after one of the whales came down the estuary as far as the railway bridge. Moby didn't respond to his signals and this morning the small group of whales was seen once more heading out to sea, probably on its way to the Azores.'

When I heard that I dropped my spoon with a clatter and put my head in my hands. I could almost feel the mud sucking and the black water pushing and then staying still, like a black lid nailed down over my head.

In the book at school there was this picture of whales when they were fast asleep. What they did was hang upside down in the water, looking like fat torpedoes with mouths. And that's what I felt like: a torpedo that's been fired and missed and got spent instead in this thick, black mud.

To make things worse, Aunty Mavis was there. She arrived real early and banged at the door and shouted through the letter box. 'Are you there, Milly? It's only me – I've to go to the bus at half-past eight and it's on your way, if I remember rightly – I thought we might walk on together.'

Chrissy bustled around fetching out a cup. There was chat about Uncle Donald's bad feet and Aunty laughing her wheezy laugh and saying stuff like: 'Keep smiling, Mill, everything's going to be fine, you'll see,' and, 'If our Ray's playing up like he is, there's not much wrong with him, I'll be bound.'

Everyone was suddenly laughing and jolly. It was as if Aunty Mavis had sat in her chair and sent out these happiness waves *zap*, like that. Even the lipstick marks on her cup were curved up in this stupid, bright-red smile.

'And what's the matter with the littlest one?' Aunty suddenly noticed me. She stretched a fat hand out over the table and tried to tickle me under my chin. You could smell some scent, a kind of flowery stuff, but I wouldn't take my head from my hands.

'He's got the hump,' our Chrissy said. 'Take no notice, he'll soon come round.'

Then Madeline hugged me and kissed my ear and said, 'Listen, pet, stop worrying, right? Dad's going to be as good as new.'

After that they carried on talking some more, acting as if everything was fine, and I wondered, what did they think they were acting *for*?

Chrissy went with me as far as the school gate and gave me this look like she does, that meant, don't you skive off school, or else! Ordinarily I wouldn't take any notice but just then I felt too bad for that, bad like when you're really upset.

We went in the classroom and got on with our sums, and Miss Gray called out the register: 'Good morning, Jimmy.' 'Good Morning, Miss Gray,' and so on until she'd been round us all.

Afterwards things went wrong again.

Miss Gray said, 'Now, children, I've got some news! You remember the children in Africa who are not lucky enough to have a school? Well, now's your chance to help them out. I'd like you each to think of what you can do, like swim a few lengths or run a mile, and then get some people to sponsor you. The money we make will go in a fund to help those children with their school.'

She said some more and then gave out some forms that said what we were supposed to do. There were gaps on the forms for sponsors to fill in. They had to write their names and where they lived, and how much money they were going to give. There was another gap for what you would do, and whether you'd done it, and where and when.

I read the form and my heart went *clunk*. I hated running, I couldn't swim, I couldn't even ride a bike. And all around me kids were flexing their muscles and puffing their chests out and talking sport: 'I'm going to swim a hundred lengths!' 'I'm going to run for three whole miles!'

Only Ben and me were quiet, and at dinner-time he jerked his head and I went after him behind the sheds.

'Listen, mate, I been thinking,' he said. 'About this sponsor thing – about what we'll do. Miss Gray never said we'd got to do stuff ourselves, I mean sporty stuff that wimps can't do. So here's my plan: we'll use the newts. What we'll do is practise making them run, and then we'll get folks to sponsor a race where everyone has to choose a newt. The one that runs farthest wins outright, and you have to pay for each newt that you choose.'

'But if people do that they'll expect something. I mean like a prize or something. Like you get when you win.'

'Yeah. Right.' Ben scratched under his bobble hat, and then shoved it further back on his head. 'So we'll give the winner a certificate, like, with the name of the winning newt on it. And the money they give us will go to Miss Gray to send to the children in Africa.'

'I don't know about that. I'll have a think. I reckon we have to let Miss Gray know what it is we're going to do.'

'Right, mate, and she'll be dead chuffed with this! There's skill in newts, see? It's not down to luck. You have to know when to tickle their tails and when it's best to leave 'em alone.'

'I'll have a think,' I said again, 'and I'll let you know what I think real soon.'

I left Ben on his own after that and took myself to the school library. I read some more about what whales did.

And that's when I nearly gave up on Deep.

Because the book said some whales *chose* to die. If food was short or something was wrong, they'd go up an estuary like ours and wait there until their hearts gave out. There was a theory (this is what the book said) that a whale would choose to do that, so as to help all the other whales. And it was no use persuading him back out to sea because he'd keep going back up the estuary, so all you could do was leave him to die.

When I read that it felt like *my* heart had given out. Deep had tricked me or I'd tricked myself, and none of us would be happy ever again.

I finished the book and threw it down, then put my coat on and went outside. In the playground kids were practising, putting markers on the ground and taking it in turns to run. Some of the girls were skipping about and counting all the skips out loud: 'I've done two hundred! That's more than you! I reckon I could do a hundred more!'

I went out of the playground and no one saw.

When I got to the harbour it was empty again. And

everywhere looked so ordinary: washing was flapping about on lines; a cat was sitting on an upturned boat. And the estuary was calm as calm. Not a ship was there. Not a bird flying. There were just some people on the railway bridge with binoculars trained out towards the sea.

I was stood looking at the water again, and knowing something other folks didn't: Deep was still there, under the waves. I didn't try to tune into him the way I had before; I just looked at the empty water with the tiny waves slapping against the wet grey stones. And it came to me then that Deep had deliberately gone somewhere I couldn't reach.

While I watched and waited the town woke up; some people were on the black gritty beach, and behind me a radio was playing too loud.

But I never moved. Not until it was time to go back home. And then I left, still with my heart like lead in my chest, scared to think Deep might have chosen to die.

13

'I'm going to do something fantastic, Dad'

I went round to Baverstock's with its sign on the door saying FRESHEST FRUIT & VEG IN TOWN.

Mam was serving a lady some brussel tops, saying, 'D'you want them under or over, my dear?'

The lady thought about it hard. In the end she said, 'I'll have 'em under, Mill, and a couple of parsnips as well, if you please.'

Some other people were queuing up, and when Mam saw me she looked surprised and said, 'Jimmy! Is it that time already? I can't get away at the moment, pet – can you go and see Dad on your own?'

I was opening my mouth to say, yeah, sure, when Baverstock yelled from out the back, 'Can you help me bag these spuds up, Mill? Soon as you've finished in the shop.'

Mam gave me another harassed look, and then took an apple off a pile. She whispered, 'Go on, love, take it – I'm owed one or two. It'll do you until you have your tea.'

I reckoned she needed cheering up, so I told her about the newt contest, and she said, 'Blow me down! That Ben of yours! (Three bananas or four today?) I reckon he'll go a very long way. But listen, ducky, you ask Miss Gray. I expect she knows you're not sporty, like. She might think of something else you can do.'

'Be blowed to that!' a customer said. 'Count me in with the newts, Mill, please! I like a flutter when all's said and done. I'll have fifty p there and back again – and let me know when it's going to take place.'

And *that* set the other ladies off: 'Give me the running order, Jim. And I'll have fifty p each way!'

In the end I left Mam taking names with Baverstock still shouting out from the back, 'The spuds are waiting! Don't be all day. And there's bags of carrots need opening.'

When I got to the hospital you could see the sun and the moon out together and the sky was this weird pigeon-wing grey, shot all over with long pink lines.

On Dad's ward the nurse was there again. She was talking to a lady with a shopping bag, saying, 'Salt! Alcohol! No Exercise! These are the things that are bad for you and sometimes they can give you a stroke.' Then she patted the lady on the arm and turned away and came up to me.

'Jimmy!' she said. 'I'm glad you've come. I think your dad's feeling better today. I reckon your visits cheer him up.

He's out of bed and he's properly dressed – he's that smart you might not recognise him!'

And *I* said, 'Our dad doesn't drink! And he's not lazy, right? What you said – that's not telling the truth! Dad's always up and doing something; you don't catch our dad sitting down.'

'What?' said the nurse. She had a label on her chest that said, *Melanie Fox. Ward Manager*. Then she gave a laugh and rubbed my head, and said, 'You've got a sharp pair of ears, Jimmy! Of course your dad's not like that at all, he's just unlucky, and that's a fact. But those things – they're not really good for you, whether you have a stroke or not.'

I stopped scowling then and walked away to where Dad was sitting on a brown plastic chair beside his bed. He was wearing a shirt with blue and white stripes and carpet slippers in red corduroy. When I came up Dad looked at me. Not straight away and not in the eye, but I saw his head turn round very slowly, and when it did, I saw something else. I saw that he looked different today. It was as if his face looked the same, but softer and younger. A hard line had gone from round his mouth and the way he was looking was quieter somehow, like a fire inside him had burnt itself out.

Dad didn't say anything to me, but he waved his good hand and then let it fall, and I felt this rush of something happening, like a flood of warm water – but better than that.

More like a window opening up, and you knowing spring is on the outside.

I pulled up a chair and sat next to Dad. Then I pinched a pear and bit into it. The juice went trickling down my chin and I said, 'Dad!' between the gloopy bites. 'You're getting better, I can tell you are!'

Dad didn't speak. He stayed real still. But his eyes had that funny spark again that came and went like a very quick blink.

'Dad, we got to do this thing at school. Something sporty and get a sponsor, you know? You can do some running or swim a bit or go on a long walk, if that's what you want. Only, me . . .' (I shrugged.) '. . . I reckon that stuff's just for the little kids.

'I'm going to do something fantastic, Dad. Like go off and do a bungee jump. Or do karate and chop everyone. Or maybe box someone bigger than me. Anyway, Dad, just so you know. In case you can't be there when it happens. I just thought I'd fill you in now, right? Only maybe I won't do any of that. Maybe I'll do something else instead. It all depends on how I feel – I mean, if I can be bothered or not. And, Dad . . .' (This is where I leant in closer.) '. . . I reckon we'd better keep it a secret and not go telling the girls or Mam.'

When I said that I finished the pear. Then I chucked the core into the bin and watched Dad thinking things with his eyes.

By then the sun had disappeared so the room was getting dark again. And perhaps it was the darkness getting to me or the funny quiet that was on the ward with just the telly chuntering out. I don't know. But something seemed to be struggling inside me, something in my head that I couldn't work out. Like a conversation going on without me, saying stuff like, why don't you tell him what's really to do? And, what'll you do when he finds out the truth?

As soon as I heard that bit of the conversation I started up again telling Dad all about myself, and some of it was true and some of it wasn't. Only it wasn't like deliberately telling a lie, it was more like kidding myself I was different and hoping that Dad might be impressed.

See, I wanted Dad to think I was great, mainly because he's so great himself. Our dad's that amazing he never seems to rest like other people, he just keeps on doing things all the while. The second he wakes up he starts doing things, even if it's only singing out loud or teasing Mam like he always does: 'Come on now, Milly, shake a leg. You're not Sleeping Beauty, you know!' You could hear him saying that first thing in the morning and afterwards he'd be busy all day, making phone calls or shopping for stuff; playing the piano down the social club.

Dad played stuff like 'Hey Jude' and 'Mull of Kintyre' and sang along as well, and you could hear him practising in our front room until Mrs Pidgeon knocked on the wall. And Dad knew people. Nearly everyone who lived round about. When he went out you could hear them calling, 'How-do, Ray? How you been, old lad?' like they were proud that Dad might be their friend.

So I told Dad things, and while I was telling them it made me feel different; more like the son Dad should have had.

After I thought that, I said, 'Dad?' and touched his arm.

And that's when Dad suddenly gave this jump and said, 'PICCALILLI!' in a big loud voice.

'What?' I said. I moved back from the bed, and Dad looked cross and said, 'PICCALILLI! PICCALILLI!' even louder and thumped on the bedspread with his good left hand.

Then a nurse came up on rubber feet and said, 'My word, Raymond, you're doing well. Now what is it that you want to say? Try speaking slowly, pet, and take your time or make a sign to say what you want.'

We both of us looked at Dad and I heard him say piccalilli again very quietly under his breath, and I was sure he didn't mean to say that, even though he knew all about sandwiches and might be thinking pickle and sardines.

I leant over Dad and stared in his face, thinking that I might somehow guess what it was he was trying to say, but Dad shut his eyes and let his hand go limp, and the nurse said, 'Come on, Jimmy, love. Your dad's done very well today but now he just needs a good long rest.'

We went down the ward and the nurse said next, 'It's

great your dad's trying to speak to you, Jimmy. A real breakthrough, no doubt about that. But listen, he'll get a lot of words wrong because his brain has lost the right connections, it can't connect words up with his mouth. But he's still got all his buttons stitched on – my word, I reckon your dad's real bright! Only, it'll take a fair time for him to get sorted out and, in the meantime, we've got to be patient a bit. We've got to be pleased with what he can do right now and try not to worry about what he can't.'

After I left Dad I went round to Ben's, although it was dark and I hadn't had my tea. Ben answered the door as soon as I knocked and I said to him, 'Right, mate. You're on with the newts.'

Ben was eating a doughnut with cream oozing out. He shoved the last of it into his mouth and slapped my right hand with his right hand and said, 'Good on you, mate! You coming in?'

'Nah. I've to have my tea.'

'Right. So long, then. See you tomorrow. That's if Barker don't see you first!'

I went home after that and by then Mam was in. 'Hello, Jimmy, pet. So how's your dad? Did you have a good chat with him tonight? I thought he was looking better today.'

I said, 'Dad was OK. He was quiet, mostly. But then he went and said "piccalilli".'

'What?' Mam stopped her drying and stared at me. 'D'you mean your dad really spoke to you? Properly, I mean? In words? Out loud?'

I nodded and Mam said, 'Piccalilli? What kind of word is that to say? He finished with his sandwich bar ages ago. Piccalilli? You'd think if he was going to speak, he might have gone and said my name!'

'The nurse said he can't say what he means.'

'Ha!' said Mam, and looked indignant. 'Piccalilli! I'll pickle him!'

She carried on drying her hands after that, and then stopped all at once and started to laugh. 'Piccalilli!' she said again. 'Of all the words for him to say!'

We were both of us laughing when the girls came in and we had to tell them what Dad had said, so then we were all of us laughing out loud, and Maddy said, 'He's getting better, Mam, just you wait. He'll be making trouble very soon!'

When I went off to bed I lay in the dark imagining stuff Dad might have said, like, 'You're just the way I was when I was a lad.' Dad was smiling because he was pleased with me, and I knew we would go off and do things together and not take either of the girls with us.

But then I thought of the stories I'd told, not really meaning to tell a lie. If Dad found out, it might perhaps make him bad again or it might make him think I was really stupid or even (and this choked me up) make him wish for a different son, a kid who was really like the lies.

So maybe I should tell him the truth before he went and found out for himself.

14
'Deep! Deep! Keep going, mate!'

Next day I woke up feeling heavy. Not in my arms and legs, the way you might think, but in my head. And I knew straight away it was Deep.

I sat at the table with my head on my hand, pretending to eat a Weetabix but really wanting to go to Deep and knowing that would be the wrong thing to do. There was an idea I had, that my wanting him to be strong again might somehow drive him further down. But it didn't stop my wanting and it didn't stop my fretting that I might never, ever see Deep again. Not alive. Not like he was when I first saw him, wild and splendid and free.

Madeline noticed the way I was and said, 'What's the matter today, Jimmy? Got the hump again?'

And I shushed her up because the news was on and Chrissy said, 'It's that whale, isn't it? Put it out of your mind, our Jim. There's nothing you can do for it. You just concentrate on Dad and school.'

With Madeline patting at my arm and Chrissy nattering on out loud, I nearly missed what the news man said, but he came on after the boring stuff.

'Moby the sperm whale has not been seen now for two days. Fears are growing that he might have died in the dirty waters of the estuary. Two divers have been searching the water for a sign of him but so far have not succeeded in locating him. The search has been halted for the time being and it is hoped that Moby will surface again soon. Should Moby have perished, the question will arise of how to dispose of him . . .'

As soon as I heard the man say that I threw my spoon down and got off my chair, and Mam said, 'Now, Jimmy, love . . .' and Madeline said,

'Let him be, Mam.'

Sometimes Maddy's not all daft, and when she said that I went in the hall and put on my coat and shouted out, 'I'm going off to school now, right? And I'm going there on my own, OK?'

Mam followed me out into the hall. She came up behind me and touched my arm. Then she gave me an apple-smelling hug and said, 'Go straight to school, Jimmy, won't you, love? Or I'll be in trouble with the Head again. And will you stop your worrying about that whale? Just think of your dad and how he is – think of him getting better again.'

I left the house and went down the road, then turned off to where the posh houses were. There was no one about. Not even anyone going off to work. But from where I was standing you could see the estuary surging on and the horizon coming down to meet the water where it went out into the open sea.

There was nothing much on the water. I couldn't even *imagine* Deep there. All you could see was the lonely water and the bridge with cars like ants on it.

After a while I turned away.

Ben was already at school when I got there. He was talking to Miss Gray. When I got close I could hear him saying, 'The thing about newts is they dance, OK? Like this . . .' Ben waved his arms around and made his eyes go big and wide. '. . . The skill comes in when you make them run. You gotta be gentle with them, see? You haven't got to make them upset or they stop. They just stay dead still and you can't shift them. To make them run you have to tease their tails, and that's what I'm telling you, right, Miss Gray? There's skill in newts. I mean, anyone can run a race but with newts you have to watch how you go.'

And I reckon Miss Gray's gone soft on Ben, because instead of saying what she would to me, like: 'You have to do something sporty yourself. Can you ride a bike or swim ten lengths?' She was giving him this mushy smile and saying brightly, 'What a good idea! Nobody else will have thought of that! But will you get anyone to sponsor the race?'

Which is where Ben suddenly turned round to me. He said, 'Jimbo here's your bloke for that. He's going to get lots of folk signed up. See, Jim's like the business side of things, while I do the really clever stuff.'

'I see! So, Jimmy, you're going to be working with Ben?'

I nodded my head without saying anything, and Miss Gray said kindly, 'Good. Right then. Let me know when the great day is. Now then, Jimmy, a word with you.'

I went with Miss Gray and stood by her desk and she said very softly, 'Where were you yesterday afternoon? Have you brought me a note from your mother, Jimmy? Or did you just take the afternoon off?'

When Miss Gray said that she wasn't smiling. Instead she was looking at me in this more-sorry-than-mad sort of way, and just for a second I thought I'd open my budget and tell her things. But I didn't. What I did was just stand there, thinking them, while Miss Gray stared and tapped her pencil and waited for me to talk out loud. In the end she answered herself. 'Well, I'll say nothing else for the moment, Jimmy. I know you've got a lot on your mind. But if it happens again, the Head will know, so try to be sensible, hey, Jimmy Wilson? And if you've got any problems, you come and tell me.'

We all of us had our lessons then and nothing much happened until playtime came round. Barker was outside with some of his mates. He was jumping around making whooping noises and flapping his hands about under his arms, when he saw me suddenly and stopped mid-flap. Then he fetched a hand out from under his arm and drew it slowly up to his chin and pulled a finger across his throat.

When he'd finished doing that he grinned and winked and carried on larking with the other kids. Then Ben slunk up and said, 'Watch it, mate, he's after you. I'd keep my head down – know what I mean?'

And up until then I'd been scared of Barker because he's bigger than me, and I'm a wimp, OK? But when Ben said that I just gave this shrug and found I meant what it said for real: I wasn't scared like I ought to be.

At home time I was setting off to see Dad. I was heading off up the mucky street when something stopped me in my tracks, only not something you could see or hear, but a kind of pull, like something at the back of your mind you are trying to remember.

I was stood there with people surging round and banging into me saying, 'Sorry, son.'

Next thing is, I'm off down the harbour and I'm *pulled* there by this invisible force. I was looking at the water with this flash of orange sun on it at a time when it's usually nearly dark. And Deep was under the orange flash. I couldn't see him properly but I knew he was there. I knew, without knowing *how* I knew, that his long, dark dream had ended and Deep had fought his way up from the pit of sleep and was slowly, slowly, moving along.

'Deep!' I shouted, and I think I was crying, and a plane was coming in to land and the noise of it swallowed up my words. 'Deep! Deep! Keep going, mate! It's not that far! Keep going, will you? I'm right with you, OK? Can you hear me? I'm right with you, Deep!'

After I said that, noise was suddenly all around. You could hear people shouting, 'The whale's back!' A photographer appeared as if by magic and instead of there being just me on the wall there were other people looking and pointing and taking snaps.

By then the sun had disappeared and a cold wind was blowing, but you could see Deep beginning to show like a black shape under the water. My heart was thudding in my chest, slowly, then faster, then faster than that, when Deep rose up in a wild rush and a spray of water shot through the air *whooosh*! *Whoosh*! *Whooosh*! Some black birds were flying into the spray and it made you think they were there on purpose, like aeroplanes flying past the Queen, and you could hear a cheer going up from the wall: 'Good old Moby! Right-on, mate!'

When that happened I went away. It was nearly dark and the street lights were on. In the alleyway you could smell people's dinners and my tummy was grumbling for something to eat, but I thought about Deep coming up again, just when everyone thought he was dead.

I thought I'd be happy if Deep woke up. It was what I had wanted and *still* wanted, right? Only instead of being happy I was something else. More a feeling like I had to watch things all the time. Not just Deep but Dad, as well, and Mam with her funny wavery smile. If I didn't stop watching, something bad might happen, and I knew that Deep wasn't really free yet and that Dad might never get properly right. So if I felt too happy or pleased with stuff, something might happen to turn it all round.

I got home without noticing, and I nearly missed something else really weird – that all the lights were on in our house.

15

'Starry, starry night'

Our house looked like it did on Christmas Eve when Dad had his mates in and Mam made them mince pies and sausage rolls. Dad would play on the organ we kept in the corner, stuff like 'The Green, Green Grass of Home' and later, when they'd had a beer, 'She'll be Coming Round the Mountain' and 'The First Noël'.

I thought suddenly, yeah! Our dad's better and he's come back home! And that thought was like a rocket behind me. I raced down the road and through the gate, nearly forgetting all about Deep. I went through the door and into the room, but instead of Dad there was Chrissy and her mates dancing around to a stupid tape. They were jumping up and down and waving their arms, and the room was full of hair and legs and you got this smell like Aunty Mavis, hot and scenty so it tickled your nose.

When I saw what was what I folded my arms and

scowled at them and carried on scowling until Chrissy noticed me and said, 'Jimmy, pet! Come here and dance!'

'Is this your brother?' A mate of hers said.

And another one said, 'Isn't he *sweet*!'

After that I was in the middle of them getting hugged and poked and lipstick-kissed. Then Mam came in wearing her best blue jeans and a T-shirt embroidered with butterflies.

'*Mam*! I said. 'What's going on?'

Mam hugged me and laughed and pulled my hair. She said, 'You've forgotten, our Jimmy, I can see you have. It's Chrissy's birthday tomorrow, pet, and she's going to the rink with some of her mates, so we're having a bit of a party tonight. We told you but maybe you didn't hear, you're that gone-out at the moment, Jim – not that I blame you. I'm gone-out myself.'

'But what about Dad?'

Mam tugged me gently into the hall. She said, 'Life has to go on you know, Jimmy, pet. We haven't forgotten about your dad. You and me'll go later on, but tonight is Chrissy's to enjoy herself.'

When Mam said that she went into the kitchen and unpacked some tangerines. 'Tunisian,' she said, 'not the best, I'll grant you that, but a present from Baverstock and that's something!'

Later Mam and me went to see Dad.

On the ward there were still some visitors, holding

hands with the people in beds and shouting very slowly and loudly, stuff like, 'MURIEL SENDS YOU ALL HER LOVE!' and, 'HOW ARE YOU OFF FOR PYJAMAS AND SOCKS?' Behind a funny curtained partition you could hear a lady yelling out loud, 'ARE YOU MANAGING TO GET TO THE TOILET, ARTHUR?' In the bed next to Dad's another lady was slowly massaging an old man's feet and speaking to him real soft and low: 'You'll be home soon, honey, you wait and see. I brought your favourite food for you – you can't eat the rubbish they give you in here.'

Dad was sitting on his own with his face turned away, and I could tell right off that he was fed-up again. He was that stiff looking and closed-in on himself you could nearly feel these vibes coming off him like tiny black needles pricking the air. If I'd been on my own I'd have sat quiet for a minute and let Dad notice me by himself, but Mam went bustling up and kissed his face and said, 'Well now, chuck, how are you tonight? You're looking better, Ray. You're on the mend. Baverstock's sent you these tangerines.'

She fussed about him, pulling his jumper and smoothing it and running a hand through his floppy hair, all the time nattering on at him brightly like he was a visitor you had to entertain.

Mam's voice was like a stream running on, pushing everything up in front of it. She didn't see Dad's tight, cold face with his mouth quirked up to one side of it or the way his good hand was clenched on his knee. Dad looked like something about to burst and I wished that Mam would just stay quiet and let Dad sort his own thoughts out.

But she didn't, and Dad *did* go and burst. He opened his mouth and shouted at her, 'BALLCOCKS! BALLCOCKS! BALLCOCKS!'

The lady massaging the old man's feet looked across at us, startled, like, then smiled and said, 'That sure is something I'd like to say!'

Which made Mam smile a small, wavery smile before she turned back again to Dad and said, 'Now then, Ray. What're you trying to say to me? Can you point to it, just to show me, like? Or maybe you could write it down? Oops! Sorry, Ray, I forgot for the moment – you can't manage to write just now. Later, maybe, when you've had some practice, that's what the therapist lady says.'

Mam said all that in one long, puffy breath, as if she couldn't wait for the words to come out, and the butterflies stuck on the front of her T-shirt twinkled and fluttered across her chest. Under the electric light the skin on her face looked white as snow, the way it does when you're going to be sick, and her eyes had a funny red rim round them as if she hadn't slept very much.

When she finished speaking Dad lay back in his chair and Mam leant over him, holding his hand. I thought I heard her say, 'I love you, Ray,' but she might have said, 'I can't hear you,' because Dad was muttering something else, something that sounded like Cocoa Cocoa, and when he'd said it, Mam said, 'Cocoa? Cocoa? That's next door's cat! Blow me down, fancy saying that! Can you say "Milly", Ray? Can you give it a try? Just for me, say "Milly", hey?'

But Dad closed his eyes and his face looked suddenly more than tired, it looked as if he had vanished inside it to somewhere you could never go.

A nurse came over to us then, and said, 'I think Raymond's tired now, Mrs Wilson. He's been trying really hard today, but you'll come back and see him tomorrow, I'm sure.'

And somehow that seemed to make me mad. Not what she was saying but the way she was talking, as if Dad wasn't there in front of us but away somewhere he couldn't see or hear.

I was right dischuffed with Mam as well. Telling Dad to keep saying 'Milly', just as if he was a budgerigar. I was going to tell her when something stopped me in the nick of time. I reckon it was Mam's face again looking like I'd not seen it before, kind of sad and empty with the chirpiness gone. And then remembering that when I talked to Dad all I did was tell him lies and maybe that was worse than Mam.

The nurse went chuntering on to us in a cheerful, too jolly kind of voice, saying stuff like, 'Don't take it to heart. It's the damage that's been done to his brain. He knows what it is he wants to say but he can't get all the right words out yet.'

She stood back smiling with her hands clasped together looking as if she was waiting for something, like for us all to be happy suddenly.

Mam gave her a smile and I took Mam's arm. Together we went on out of the ward and into the clear starry night. We were walking along slowly, arm in arm, when I stopped on the pavement and looked at the stars, way above us in the navy blue sky, just hanging there and glittering.

'What's the matter?' Mam said, surprised.

And I said, 'Nothing. Just the stars. They remind me somehow of Dad, that's all.'

Mam looked up and gave a chuckle. Her nose was pointing up at the sky and she said, 'D'you remember that time he got us out of bed to see some star he'd not seen before? A flaming great thing he said it was, and we were all out of bed in our pyjamas, gaping up at the sky like lemons . . .'

'And it turned out to be an aeroplane going on quietly with its engine off, then it suddenly started up again!'

'Instead of feeling stupid your dad just laughed and started singing out there in the garden, "Starry, starry night . . ." until Mr Pidgeon knocked on the window and told him to put a sock in it!'

Mam and me laughed and hugged each other at the thought, and then went home to Chrissy and her mates and ate some cake that Mam had made, and I went to my room to make Chrissy a card.

I drew a star and coloured it in and put some glittery stuff on it. Then I got into bed and closed my eyes and had this dream that was all about stars. But the stars were strange. There were lots of them flaring with this bright white light, dazzling they were, like fireworks.

And that's not all. Because the stars weren't just stars like you usually see them, in the sky and a long way off. They were much bigger and brighter and grander than that, and each of the stars had a face on it.

And each of the faces was like our dad's.

16
'Sometimes whales will choose to die'

In the morning I was up early, right? It was Saturday and I was anxious to go and see Deep. I got up before the news came on, and I ate a banana that was going soft and then left Chrissy's card on the kitchen table with a present I'd made her – nothing much – just a box made out of cardboard and glue decorated with a pattern of shells that she could keep her bits and pieces in.

After that I'd have been out the door, but Mam came down in her dressing-gown. She looked tired like she did in the hospital, but maybe it was the light again. Her dressing-gown had a hole in it and the hem was frayed with bits hanging down. She said, 'Well now, Jimmy, couldn't you sleep? I thought I heard someone moving around. Are you going out, pet? At this time of day? It's that whale again, isn't it? You're worried about it – but listen, Jimmy – you shouldn't be. There's nothing you can do for it, chick

– why don't you put it out of your mind?'

Mam meant well but she thought that Deep was going to die. She didn't actually say it out loud but I understood well enough how she thought. Mam was trying to save me from getting hurt and somehow that made me feel right soft, so I gave this shrug and said, 'Ballcocks!' meaning to go and make her laugh. But I said it wrong and it came out gruff and Mam stared at me for one long moment and then said,

'All right then, pet. You go if you must.'

She turned away and I went back to the door, but I didn't feel right about going then, so I waited a while, just shuffling my feet, and then I said, 'Mam – I didn't mean to say that. I just thought it might go and tickle you, like.'

Mam turned back and gave me a closed-up smile. 'I know that, pet, it just shook me, that's all – now don't you go stopping out too long. It's cold and you've already been poorly once. I'd best get going – I'm in early today. Baverstock's expecting a busy morning and I've to help him set the trestles up.'

I went down to the harbour and it was light by then, but cold. Rain was falling and it got down your neck and made chickenpox marks on the dark grey water. I'd expected to be on my own but all the news men were back again. Their cigarette smoke was curling up into the air and they were joking about and stamping their feet. One of them blew dead hard on his hands and then spoke into a microphone:

'. . . Thank you, John. Yes, Moby the sperm whale set off yesterday and was seen heading down towards the sea. So far Moby has been spotted moving under the road bridge and going slowly towards the railway bridge. He was seen briefly on the far side of the railway bridge and then vanished under the polluted waves of the estuary. It is believed that workmen on the bridge may have alarmed Moby and sent him diving for cover. Sperm whales have excellent hearing and strange sounds may be confusing or cause sudden panic.

'For the first time in history a merchant ship has stopped voluntarily in order to allow Moby time to recover. We are all rooting for Moby but, of course, as time goes on he will become weaker and then the outlook for him will be very bleak indeed.'

I looked out over the water. I knew that Deep was back in the mud and that he'd gone there of his own accord.

Sometimes whales will choose to die.

I was looking at the water but feeling something inside my head, a kind of darkness I hadn't felt before, not even when Deep was going to sleep. The darkness was spreading like a long black shadow, it was squeezing out the daylight and the grotty harbour wall so that soon there was just this blackness and Deep. I was inside Deep's body, I was inside his head. I was in the blackness when I felt Deep move. I moved my own legs at the same time, but they were dragging and heavy, as heavy as lead, and my heart was just this one, slow beat.

Something happened after that: not a thought or a movement; more as if Deep's head was suddenly clear and he knew what it was he had to do.

Immediately, there was this roaring noise, a dark pull like a headache coming, and then a great slapping surge of water.

Suddenly, I was back inside myself but dazzled by this burst of light. When the dazzle died down I could see the harbour and it looked the same as it always looked.

I could see Deep as well. He was out of the water and beginning to swim, and at first I thought, Yes! He's getting away, he's going to join his mates out at sea.

But Deep wasn't travelling out to sea. He was coming back down the estuary again, past the island in the middle and past the bridges, to the shallowest, dirtiest part of the water, back to where he would surely die. Deep was moving very slowly, rising gently out of the water and letting it carry him down again.

And nobody made the smallest sound.

Even the rain stopped falling and the water was like a smooth grey sheet. People were stood on the harbour wall and they were watching him go as if they were watching themselves go slowly, slowly towards their end.

When I saw what Deep was doing I waited a while and then turned away. I ran and ran as hard as I could. Not anywhere in particular, just running because I had to do it, even though I didn't know where or why.

17
Tickling newts

I finished up at Ben's house again, mainly for something normal to do. His mam opened the door to me and said, 'Ben's just finishing his breakfast, pet. He's got a delicate tummy, you know. Little bits and often, that's what the doc said. Now tell me, Jimmy, how's your dad today?'

'OK, I s'ppose.' I shrugged my shoulders and looked down at my feet. I didn't want to talk to her about Dad because he was my secret, the same as Deep, and talking about him just wouldn't feel right.

When Ben came up he was eating a cake covered all over in dark chocolate cream. 'Wotcher,' he said, licking cream off his mouth. 'You coming out to the shed with me?'

Ben kept his newts in a tank in the shed. When you went in you got this newty smell, like fish only not as strong as that. The newt tank was like another planet. Bushes were in it, all spiky and stiff. Pebbles and boulders and sandy craters, and a pond in the middle for the newts to drink.

We were just going out the back door to the shed when Ben's Mam came running up behind. 'Ben!' she said. 'You're not going out there? You'll catch your death and you've not finished eating – there's a muffin if you want it, pet. Chocolate chip, the sort you like best.'

''S OK, Mam. Got some business to do. I'll have me muffin a bit later on when I have me cocoa – say, eleven?'

'Well, put this on if you're going out there – and, Jimmy – don't keep him out too long, his chest's not been right since he were a tot.' Ben's mam plonked a woolly hat on his head and pulled it down to cover his ears, then she tightened the scarf up round his neck while Ben just stood there grinning at her.

When she'd finished we went off to the shed and Ben snapped the light on and went to the tank. You couldn't actually see any newts – they blended in with the rocks and sand – but Ben said, 'There's old Dandy – she's a real doer – run 'er legs off if you treat her right, and that one's Beano. He's a bit slower but he gets there in the end all right.' He tapped on the glass and two twigs in the tank started moving about. Ben took the lid off the tank and picked the newts up. He stroked them gently with the tip of his finger and then gave me one to hold.

'People think newts got no feelings but I'm telling you, mate, they got it wrong. Newts like you to give them a bit of fuss. They *appreciate* it. They like you to tickle them under the throat.'

The newt in my hand was smooth as silk with tiny feet and bright black eyes. Ben put his newt back in the tank and fiddled around under a spiky bush. He fetched two more newts out for me to see. 'This is Linda,' he said, stroking her. 'I reckon she'll cop for some babies soon. And this is Santa – get it? He's a bit more pink. Santa's lazy; you have to coax him along. And those are Puddle and Cotton in there. They're young yet, so we'll have to see how they go.'

The newts all looked the same to me, but Ben took them out and stroked each one and then set them down on a bench in the shed. 'We'll have a dummy run today. Just to get them in training, see? The goalpost is this plant pot here. We'll line 'em all up and then tickle their tails.'

Ben lined the newts up very carefully and then stood back and squinted at how they looked. 'You tickle Dandy and Linda and Cotton, and I'll do the others – are you ready? Get set!'

Ben started to tickle the tails of his newts and they began to move along very slowly with Ben speaking to them in this daft, cooing voice: 'Yeah – great! Come on, Beano! Show 'im what you can do, me old mate! Get on with it, Santa, you've a race to run!'

I tickled the tails of a couple of newts but, instead of starting to move away, they just stood where they were and blinked their black eyes. One of them lifted a claw off the bench and stood on three legs like some stupid newt statue.

'Yer not tickling right, yer too heavy, see? Newts like handling carefully. They're delicate. You got to make your fingers dead light and thin, and that's what I was telling Miss Gray – there's skill in newts. They take practising.'

'Yeah. Well.' I shrugged at Ben. 'They're your newts. Maybe they don't like me.'

Ben stopped his tickling and flashed a look up. His face was red from all the excitement and when I said what I did it went redder still, 'Yer wrong there, mate, but that's another thing! Newts have got to know you like them, same as what I was telling you now – newts are like people, they got feelings, see?'

'Maybe I'll find something else to do.'

'Oh yeah? Like what? You can't go back on what you said. It's business, right? So you can't do that. Anyway, you've forgotten something. We're wimps, we are. We don't do sport and stuff.'

He turned away huffed and carried on fiddling about with his newts, and after a minute I said, 'Right. OK. I'll come back soon and have another go, but I can't stop now, got something to do. Anyway, your mam's looking out the window – I reckon your cocoa's just about done.'

When I left Ben's house it was still real early, and I'd told him a lie about having something to do. I just didn't want to do newts then. And neither did I want to go back home. Chrissy'd be there and Maddy, as well, and they'd likely be giggling about with their mates.

I didn't want to go and see our dad, either. Somehow Deep's moving back up the estuary and Dad's clenched fist on his knee had got all mixed up together, almost like they were the same bad thing, and there was nothing I could do that would make any difference to either of them.

I went down the road and had a think, and I remembered the sponsors. I thought who else I could get on the list. Straight away the Pidgeons' name cropped up. I thought they'd be good for fifty p, and I was the business side of things, so I went home and crept in the house dead quiet and got the bit of paper out of my room. Then I went next door, past the bad-tempered lions and a sign on the gate that said, *Shimolee*. The curtains at the windows were all drawn back so I reckoned they must be up and about. Then I rang the bell and stepped back a pace and waited for someone to answer the door.

18
'All at once he started to cry'

It was a while before anyone came, so I stood on this mat with a picture of a cat that said WELCOME along the top of it. I was squinting through the frosted glass at the fuzzy blur in the hall, trying to make out if they were in or not. The blur stayed like it was, just brown and grey, so I rang again and folded my arms. And nothing much happened again.

I might have gone after that except I heard a noise inside somewhere, like a door being opened, and then the fuzzy brown got lighter. I heard somebody cough and the sound of feet and then the bolt being pulled back on the door. The door opened a crack with the chain still on it and Mrs Pidgeon's face appeared.

'Yes?' she said, suspiciously. Then she saw who it was and instead of looking pleased or relieved she looked even more suspicious. 'Is something wrong with Mummy?' she said. 'Or is it Daddy? Has he got worse?'

'No,' I said, and I was getting right cross with her by then. 'I got to do this thing for school. It's a race, sort of, and people are s'posed to sponsor you, right? For the kids in Africa, so that they can have a school like ours. It's fifty p, or more if you like, and if you want to do it you've to sign this form.'

'Oh,' she said, and smiled a bit, as if the smile really hurt her face. 'Well. I shall have to ask Mr Pidgeon about that. You might as well come and wait in the lounge.'

She turned round and I went after her into the living-room. There was a smell of something – polish, maybe – and Mrs Pidgeon's lounge looked different to ours. It had the same window – it was the same shape and size and all, but it didn't look like ours. It had swirly brown carpet and a three-piece suite, and you could tell the Pidgeons weren't used to kids because of the stiff, neat way it looked, and the fiddly ornaments everywhere.

Mrs Pidgeon saw me looking at them and said, 'Don't touch anything, will you, dear?' Then she left the room and went in the kitchen, and I heard her say to Mr Pidgeon, 'It's that boy from next door. He wants money for something. Can you see to it, Keith? He's such an odd sort of boy.'

After that there was a gap, then Mr Pidgeon came striding in. 'Now then, young man,' he said, 'what's all this?'

'It's a race, like,' I said, 'you've to get sponsors for. It's for children in Africa. To build them a school.'

'A race now, is it? I'll go for that. I was something of a runner myself. How far have you to run, then, Jimmy me lad?'

That's when I told him about the newts. I was telling him while Mrs Pidgeon came in and sat down on the edge of a chair, and I saw the smile on her face slip away and her mouth crumple up to a small black hole.

'Newts!' she said, when I finished my chat. 'I don't know about that, do you, Mr Pidgeon? Nasty, slimy, smelly things. Ugh! I don't think I could sponsor a newt.'

'Newts are grand! They're special, see? And they're not slimy, they're smooth as silk. Newts are delicate, they take skill, do newts. There's nothing wrong with newts, OK?' My voice had gone too loud-sounding and my face was getting red.

Then Mr Pidgeon said, 'I'll handle this,' and he came up and slapped me on the back and said in a daft sort of matey voice, 'Newts, eh? Well, that makes a change. How much have the others pledged? Right then, I could match them on that. Now, Mrs Pidgeon, what about it? Will you have a flutter the same as me?'

And Mrs Pidgeon put a hand to her throat and said, 'No, Keith, thank you. I don't hold with that.'

Mr Pidgeon gave me this giant wink and said, 'Women – I ask you! They do have their ways!'

He signed the form and I was on my way out when

Mrs Pidgeon said, in a too polite voice, 'Will Daddy be back at business soon?'

'Our dad cleans houses!' I yelled at her. 'That's what he does! We're proud of him and he's good at it. He gets lots of people ringing him up!'

'Well, then. Yes. Quite. I'm sure,' Mrs Pidgeon spoke without moving her lips because her mouth was scrunched up in a hole again.

After that Mr Pidgeon showed me out and before the door closed I heard *her* say, 'Such a rude boy – but still – what can you expect . . .?'

Which made me want to go back home and see Maddy and Chrissy and have a chat with them, and maybe even give them a hug. Only they weren't in the house like they were supposed to be. Instead there was a note on the kitchen table that said, *Gone Shopping. Back at Dinner. Thanks for Box – Just What I Want! Don't Mess About While You're on Your Own. BE GOOD!!*

And it's likely I felt lonely then. As if I wanted someone to play with who wasn't Ben, another friend to tell things to and maybe have a laugh. But that's the trouble with being a wimp, most of the time you're on your own, except for girls who want to boss you around or treat you like you was just a nipper, and straighten your clothes and comb your hair. Not for the first time I wished I was bigger. Being bigger meant you were tougher, right? You could kick a ball with both your feet and jump a fence without falling off.

Then the telephone rang and made me jump. On the answerphone, a lady's voice came puffing out: 'Mr Wilson? Ray? Deborah here. (Brian, will you please stand *still*!) Sorry I haven't been in touch, but, you know . . . I was wondering if you're better yet? Only (Brian, will you stop that *now*.) I need to go shopping and Dave's away, and you're the only one who can manage Brian. Give us a buzz. Hope you don't mind. Well, that's all for now – tarra, Raymond. Hope to hear from you very soon.'

Which made me want to go and see Dad.

I got there earlier than I'd been before. People were still doing things on the ward, but Dad's bed was empty and so was his chair. Even his slippers had gone from under the bed and so had a lot of the mouldy fruit. If it weren't for the notice up over his bed saying MR RAYMOND GEORGE WILSON I might have thought he'd gone and left, and I was standing there wondering what to do when the lady visiting at the next bed said, 'Don't you worry, darling, he's OK. He's gone to physio with a beautiful girl. My! You should've seen the smile on his face!'

Probably I looked puzzled then, because the lady gave a great big laugh and said, 'He's gone to do exercises, sweetheart – did you think your dad had run away? You go down the ward, through the door on your right – and knock, mind you, before you go in or you never know what you might find!'

She gave another crackly laugh and slapped a hand across her knee, and laughed again when I answered her back. 'Dad reckons he's enough with the girls at home. He says they're not like girls should be – three women in the house, that's what he says, and he still has to go and mend his own shirts!'

'Is that so? Well now! Your dad looks smart to me!'

The lady was still laughing when I went down the ward and through the door on the right like she said. I didn't bother knocking but that didn't matter because all Dad was doing was playing with cups. There were red cups and blue cups and bright yellow cups, all made out of shiny plastic, and Dad was very slowly moving them round. His bad arm was up in front of him and when he used his good arm he gave this grunt, and the lady who was with him said, 'That's good, Raymond. Take your time. That's it! You're doing fine.' Then she saw me come in and she gave this smile and said, 'You must be Jimmy. What a face! You're the spitting image of your dad. Come in, sweetheart, and give him a kiss. Your dad's doing really well today.'

I went in slowly if you want to know. I went in slowly because our dad didn't look like Dad. He didn't look like *anyone's* dad. He looked like a grown-up kid playing about with the stupid cups and not being able to get it right. As well as that he looked smaller somehow, hunched up on the edge of the bed.

I was looking at Dad and thinking that, when all at once he started to cry. Great big sobs came out of him and glittery tears ran down his face. I'd never seen my dad cry before and it made me feel like I was suddenly a very old man and my dad was the one you'd to look-out for. I thought as well that I'd made him cry, just by the power of my thoughts.

'Dad,' I said, and might have said some more but suddenly I was crying, too. Crying for Dad and for me and for Deep, and for Mam working down at Baverstock's. Once I'd started crying I couldn't stop, and there was me and Dad crying like that, not knowing for sure what we were crying *for*.

Then the lady put an arm round me. 'Cheer up, pet,' she said, 'it's not your fault. It's just the way your dad is now. He cries and he laughs as easy as *that* – ' she snapped her fingers in front of my nose '– and it's likely he doesn't know why he cries. It's just his brain playing tricks on him.'

If I could have believed what the lady said, I would. But it seemed to me that Dad was crying all his sadness out and when he finished crying there'd be nothing much left, just this person who used to be Dad and somehow wasn't any more.

That made me cry even harder than ever and the lady said, 'Why don't you go and give Dad a hug?' She gave me a shove that sent me halfway across the floor. And very slowly I went up to Dad. Without saying anything I touched his hand, then I sat down next to him on the bed and leant my head against his arm. Dad smelt of the hospital, of starch and food and the disinfectant that goes on the floor. We were sitting like that, with my head on his arm, both of us feeling a bit awkward and stiff with the lady looking at what we were doing.

But the weird thing was, we both stopped crying and this funny quiet came into the room. Then slowly Dad's good hand came into mine, and the lady said, 'There now. That's better isn't it, Jimmy?'

After that I went back to wait on the ward, and the lady visiting the next bed said, 'Sweetheart, you look like you need a treat,' and then *she* came across and gave me a hug.

Later on Dad came back to his bed, but instead of just sitting there he pushed his hand out towards me again. And the way he pushed it, it looked like it hurt; dead slow it was, an inch at a time. When it got to me I held it fast and Dad said, 'Smurffit,' (it sounded like that) and I said, 'Smurffit,' back to him.

And maybe that's what made me laugh. I don't mean Dad not saying his words, but the way we could say things that made no sense and still understand what we both meant.

'Smurffit!' I said again, out loud. 'Ballcocks to you and piccalilli!'

'Smurffit!' Dad said back to me, and the quirky side of his face went up and this noise like a laugh came wheezing out: 'Hmm hmm hm hm hm.'

And that made me laugh out loud again, so me and Dad were making this noise – *ha ha ha* and *hm-hm-hm* – until a nurse came up and said, 'What's to do?' and then *she* started laughing and the lady at the next bed joined in, slapping her leg and wiping her eyes and saying, 'That's the funniest thing I've heard all week!'

A while after that it went quiet again. I think that Dad had tired himself out because of all the fun he'd had, so I took myself off home and when Chrissy came back she gave me a hug and said, 'Jimmy Wilson! I do love you! Will you have some birthday cake now, pet?'

19
Bimbly glove

Monday started the way Mondays usually do in our house: we'd all got up too late; we'd run out of bread; I was in the way. And it was raining.

Chrissy was shouting at me, 'Jimmy! Have you nicked my pen?' and I was yelling back, 'Why pick on me?' which was the wrong thing to say because she had me then: 'Because you nick things all the time! You had my pencils yesterday and broke the point off my only good one.'

I guess I must have shrugged at her, mostly because she was dead right, and that made her even madder still: 'You can take that look off your face, our Jimmy, or you'll be sorry – real sorry – I'm telling you!'

She was yelling that when the news came on and without even thinking I said, 'Sshush, Sshush,' which made Chrissy say to me, 'I'll shush you!' She switched off the radio and stamped out the room and I got off my chair and switched it back on. Suddenly I couldn't eat any more.

'Despite repeated attempts to usher him out to sea, Moby the sperm whale has returned to the estuary and is now believed to be somewhere between the road and the railway bridges. There seems little hope that Moby will survive; it is now over a week since he first took the wrong turning and Moby has been short of food and the deep, clean water which he needs for his continued survival. It is feared that Moby is completely disorientated by his surroundings and will no longer be able to make the journey back to the open sea.

'Discussions are taking place as to the best method to dispose of Moby when he dies. The most favoured option is to use dynamite to blow up the body, but it is not yet certain what will happen . . .'

My head went blank. I couldn't hear Chrissy slamming about or Mam moaning on about Baverstock, and I wasn't with Deep either, although I wanted to be. When he chose to come back down the estuary, that's when he chose to be on his own. I couldn't get near to him any more. He was alone the way he wanted to be, sinking slowly towards his death.

I was sat in my chair and my heart was aching with a real pain. Then Mam came over and put her arms round my neck and kissed the top of my head. 'I'm sorry, Jimmy,' she said softly.

I stood up to go on my stiff legs, and she said, 'Come and

see me after school. If I can get off early we'll have a treat. We'll get fish 'n' chips from Doughty's, hey? Don't upset yourself, Jimmy, love.'

I went outside, and the worse thing was I couldn't even make a wish for Deep.

When I got to school there was no sign of Barker, but Ben was there with his red hat on. 'I've had a word with 'em,' he said, 'so they'll make more effort with you next time. Newts like you to tell 'em stuff, you know? It makes them happy, and if they're happy they do what you want them to do.'

'S'pose so,' I said.

I was fed up with Ben and his stupid newts and he got huffy with me the way he does and said, 'Trouble is, you don't *appreciate* them.'

After that we went inside. We did our sums to get settled down and then Miss Gray said, 'Right now, children, it's time we opened the suggestion box.'

There's this box, see, that she keeps on her desk, and it's there for you to put things in, like stuff you might want her to tell you about or books you've read that you thought were good. Every so often she opens the box and reads out loud what you've put in there, and then we all decide what we're going to do.

'Aha!' said Miss Gray when she took the lid off. 'I see we've got some paper in here. That's smashing, children, now let me see . . .'

She opened the first bit of paper up and said, 'Thank you, Sally. We will all read this book – have you got it with you so we can look? Thank you, you can leave it with me. It's a book about lions in Africa, so I think it will fascinate us all.'

She opened the second paper. 'Christopher, thank you, dear. Yes we can talk about buses sometime, if that's what you really want to do.'

The third piece of paper was put there by Ben. 'Newts!' said Miss Gray. 'I think we've got a book about newts. No, dear, no need to bring them in.'

That's when she got to the fourth piece of paper. What she did was take it out and open it and carefully smooth it down. Then her eyebrows went right up and she said, 'This suggestion isn't funny *at all*! Which of you is responsible for it? No one? Well, when I find out, it will mean *trouble* for someone and that's for sure. Now stop talking and get on with your sums.'

When she said that Miss Gray looked at me and crooked a finger to call me over. I was stood there at the side of her desk and from where I was standing I could see the paper. On it in big red letters it said, *JIMMY WILSON – MEGA WIMP!! Suggestion – why don't you feed him to Moby the whale??*

Reading that made me think that Miss Gray might feel sorry for me because I was a wimp, and instead of being pleased I was angry.

I was stood there with my arms folded and Miss Gray

swivelled round to me on her chair. We were eye to eye and nose to nose and Miss Gray said, 'Now then, Jimmy, what's all this? Do you know who's giving you a hard time? Can you tell me, Jimmy? You should, you know. I don't care for this sort of thing at all and I want to stamp it out if I can.'

From where I was standing I could see myself reflected in Miss Gray's brown eyes, small like a pinhead and a long way off.

And the bad thing is, I nearly told her. The good thing is, I didn't. Not just because I didn't want to grass on Barker but more because I wanted to stick up for wimps. See, being a wimp means you don't do sport and stuff mainly because you don't *want* to do it, because there's other things you'd rather do, and that's all it means. That was one of the reasons I didn't say anything; the other reasons were Dad and Deep. I wanted them to be proud of me.

Deep was still in my head like a friend or a brother, even though I wasn't connected to him the way I knew I had been before. And I didn't want to let him down. I had the idea that he would somehow know what I was up to, even if he had died in the estuary.

So I said to Miss Grey, or shouted, more like, 'I wouldn't tell you if I knew! Leave me alone, will you? I'm fed up with you!'

Behind me I could hear the other kids mutter, and then

this gap when they went dead quiet and waited to see what would happen next.

I saw Miss Gray open her mouth then close it again and wait while she thought of something else to say. In a moment she said, 'All right, Jimmy. I understand. You can go back to your desk now and get on with those sums.'

I did what she said and nothing much happened for the rest of the day, apart from Ben coming up and hissing at me, 'I'm thinking of sticking up for you, right? Just as soon as I've got rid of me cold.'

At tea-time I went straight round to see Dad.

He was on the chair at the side of the bed and as soon as he heard me coming in he turned round to look and his face quirked up. When I sat down next to him his hand came out and I took a hold of it and we sat like that.

'Smurffit,' I said, and Dad said, 'Smurffit,' back, and 'Thrumpit' and 'Piccalilli,' still with his face all quirking up.

After that I started telling Dad things. Stuff about Mam and the girls and that, and stuff about what I'd been doing in school. Then I waited a minute for him to reply, but he didn't, so I told him about the newts. 'Ben and me, we're racing them, see? The other stuff, I mean swimming and that, that's more for the little kids, right? Me and Ben, we're too old for that, we're too clever for it, so we're doing the newts.'

Dad just stayed quiet, looking at me. He didn't try to say

anything back, instead, he gave my hand a squeeze. Only, not a squeeze where you grip real tight but more like he was stroking my hand. I could tell he wasn't smiling then, but he was listening to me very hard, almost as if he'd not heard me before.

So then I told him all about Barker, but not the real truth like it was, just the stuff I wanted to tell. I said, 'Barker played this trick on me. He put a daft suggestion in the box at school and that made Miss Gray really mad. She asked me if I knew who did it and I said 'no' to her, straight off. I said it because of how things are, because this is just between Barker and me. I reckon we'll have a showdown soon and he'll wish he hadn't mixed with me then.'

I was talking to Dad and I was getting this really weird feeling. Like I was talking myself out of who I was, so I was still Jimmy Wilson, all right and tight, but I wasn't; I was this other kid as well, the kid who I talked about to Dad.

And that set me off thinking again. Stuff like, what if everyone was the same as me? What if everyone was more than one person: the person they wanted to be, inside their head, and the person who they really were?

When I thought that I gave this sigh and took my hand away from Dad's. And Dad said something that sounded like my name. 'Bimbly,' was what it came out like. 'Bimbly glove, Bimbly glove.'

I got up to go soon after that because I wanted to have

some fish 'n' chips, and I was nearly out in the corridor when I stopped where I was and had another think. Then I marched right back to where Dad was and leant over him and said dead fast, 'Dad – what I tell you – it might not be true,' and then I went off to go and find Mam.

Deep was on the telly that night. Up until then I'd never watched the news because it was as if being on a film meant he didn't just belong to me.

He came on right at the very end. In the film Deep was rising out of the water and he was doing it in slow motion while the newsreader said that he was going to die.

And even Chrissy went quiet. There was me and Mam and Chrissy and Maddy, all watching Deep, with the man talking. When he finished nobody said anything. Nobody told me it would be all right. Nobody told me not to care. We just switched the telly off and sat quiet and still, and stayed like that until we went to bed.

20
'You're a great bloke, Jimmy'

Next day I didn't go near the harbour. I didn't want to see the empty water where Deep should be or, worse still, Deep's death. But I could sense stuff going on. People on the street seemed glummer than usual. You got the idea that even though nobody said it out loud they were waiting for Deep to die and for things to go back to normal again.

At school it was hard to settle down. Kids kept chuntering to each other and getting told off. I got all my sums wrong again and broke the vase with pussy willow in, and Miss Gray said, 'Jimmy, what's the *matter* with you?'

At break-time Barker came sauntering up. 'How you doing, Jimbo? Fancy a fight, or are you too scared?'

And you know what? I couldn't even be bothered with him, so I let him carry on like that and just shrugged and kicked some gravel about. And that seemed to really make him mad, because he suddenly gave my shoulder a thump and said, 'Right then, wimp. I'll be seeing you again straight after school.'

School went on as usual after that until it was time to go home. Then Ben came up while I was putting my coat on and said, 'Listen, mate. Barker's outside just hanging about, and I reckon as how he's waiting for you. If I was you I'd stay in here and go out with the teachers, like.'

After he spoke Ben pulled a handkerchief out of his pocket and blew his nose and coughed dead loud. He put the hanky away again and said, 'I told our mam I'd go straight home, otherwise I'd help you, right? But if you go outside here's what you should do: tell Barker to mind his own. Tell him, like, to stop bothering you or you'll tell your mam and *she'll* sort 'im out. That's what I'd do if I was you.'

Ben put his hat on and pulled it down and picked his bag up off the floor. 'So long then, mate. I'll be seeing you later on, I expect, for a bit more training with me newts.'

When Ben left I went outside and I wasn't especially scared. I expect I was too full of sadness for that, as if I'd never smile again.

I went down the road and Barker was there, where you couldn't see him from the school gates. He was hanging around with two of his mates and blocking the path deliberately, 'Here he comes!' I heard one of them yell. 'Let's get him, quick! Let's stick 'im one on!' They were grinning across their stupid faces and jumping up and down and waving their arms. Barker had his fists clenched up and was coming towards me punching the air.

Ordinarily I'd have been petrified, Barker being so big and all, but get this, will you, I *still* wasn't scared.

'Pack it in, Barker,' I said in this fed-up voice. 'I can't be bothered with you just now. Beat me up tomorrow, OK?'

And that's when Barker threw this punch – *blam*! *Splat*! – across my nose and I went down *smack*, with my face running blood and Barker's over me with his fist up again, when suddenly *he's* knocked to the ground.

Whack! 'Take that!' I heard a voice say. 'You bully, you! He's only small!' *Whack*! *Bang*! A bag went down on Barker's head and his mates were off running down the street.

And it would have to be our Chrissy, right? Coming this way home from her school on purpose to go round to Mam's with me. She sees Barker have a go at me but she doesn't see that I don't care – and what does she do? She knocks him down and sends him sprawling on the mucky pavement, and then gives him a kick when he's lying there.

I could feel my face start to crimson up. To have your big sister fight for you! I'm telling you, I'd not felt so soft, not *ever* in my life before!

Chrissy bent down to help me up. Dead kind she was, just chattering on, stroking the hair from off my face and spitting on a hanky to wipe the blood.

And Barker sat sprawled on the ground all the time,

watching it happen with this grin on his face, making sure to take everything in, so he'd be able to blab at school the next day.

'I'm *all right,* Chrissy,' I shouted out. 'Just leave me alone. I can handle Barker. I don't need you to go sorting him!'

'Oho! Don't you now? Well, it looks like it! You should see the state of your face, our Jimmy. What would Mam say if she saw you like this?'

Chrissy tossed her hair back from her face and carried on wiping while I gave a shrug and looked at the ground without saying anything. That made her more excited than ever. She said, 'Honestly, Jimmy! Talk about trouble! It seems to follow you around. Stand still, will you, and don't muck about. Our mam's got enough on her plate as it is, without having to fret about you all the time.'

What Chrissy was saying wasn't all true and it wasn't fair, either. But it still made me feel like I'd got it all wrong, as if I couldn't be sad for Dad and for Deep as well in case there wasn't enough sadness in me to go round.

We got to Baverstock's without saying much else, just, 'Excuse *me,*' and stuff like that if we accidentally walked too close.

Mam was busy serving a lady with a posh grey suit and a voice that sounded like nails in her mouth: 'Ai'll hev wun of those and some reddishes, please – are they local, do you know?'

'Nah,' said Mam, 'too early yet. These are Spanish, grown on too fast – not got the bite in 'em properly, yet.'

'Ai see,' the lady said, put out. 'Hwhat do you recommend, may I arsk?'

'Beetroot!' said Mam. 'Boiled right here. Plenty of vitamins and the like in that. And spinach – that'll put some hairs on your chest.'

Up until then I'd never heard anyone say the aitch in 'what' before and I guess Chrissy hadn't either, because we were both staring at the lady as if she had two heads, and Mam gave us a wink behind her back and said, 'Will that be hall for today, Madam?'

When the lady left Mam said, 'Right, you two. Give me half a mo' and I'll be right with you – Baverstock owes me an hour or so.'

Mam went in the back and then came out fast with her coat on and a bulging bag. 'Come on, quick! Baverstock's out the back right now and what he don't see won't hurt him much.'

We went down the road and I took Mam's bag and she said, 'What you been up to, Jimmy, love? Did you fall down? I don't know! I'm always telling you to fasten your shoes, but will you listen? No, you won't!'

I opened my mouth to say what was what and then saw the look on Chrissy's face, a look that said to me clear as clear, don't you go worrying Mam, our Jimmy, or you'll be getting a thick ear from me!

So I shrugged a bit and then said, 'Yeah. Right. Sorry, Mam.'

Which made Chrissy give my arm a squeeze and the three of us carried on walking like that, with Chrissy pleased and Mam dead chuffed because she managed to escape from Baverstock, and me with this stupid cut on my face, fed up with Chrissy, but chuffed as well because I managed to keep my mouth shut tight.

The day went on all right after that, because when we got to the ward our dad was there, and you could tell straight away he was feeling better. He was sat on his chair and he was looking for us. In the window you could see the sun setting, with Dad's head a round shape in front of it. A streak of pink sun went across his mouth and it made you think he was smiling at us, or just that he was happy for once.

'Well, Ray, you're looking chipper today.' Mam went up and kissed him, and Chrissy an' all, and the pink streak ran further over his face.

Then *I* went up and said, 'Smurffit, Dad,' and smacked my left hand against his left hand.

Dad quirked his mouth and said, 'Smurrfit,' back. Mam said, 'I can see you two been up to no good.' She unpacked her shopping bag and gave him the bananas in a great big bunch. 'Canary. Small. But they taste like bananas, I'll say that for them. And this here celery – it's good today – you could get the nurse to give you some later. And maybe the gentleman in the next bed. He looks like he's a celery man.'

Perhaps it was Dad looking that much brighter or the late sun making us all feel warm, but it's like we were a family again and I was listening to the others talk. It felt as if Dad was coming back. As if that bit of him that had gone away had really been there all the time, only we hadn't been able to see it before.

Then Dad's hand crept out to me and very slowly touched my face close to the bit that Barker had whacked. 'Bimbly?' he said, 'Bimbly, glove?'

And I was nearly tempted to tell him a lie, the way I did when I talked before, just to show him how special I was, but there was Chrissy glaring across the bed and Mam busy arranging fruit. So in the end I said, 'I fell over, Dad. My shoes were undone. They made me trip.' Another lie, I know that all right, but a lie that somehow seemed more like a truth, although I couldn't fathom out why.

Then Chrissy said, 'You're a great bloke, Jimmy,' with a smile in her voice. Nobody ever said that to me before, but it seemed likely now I heard it out loud, so I decided to believe it straight away.

If that's all that had happened it would still have been good. But before we left there was something else. Mam was reaching over Dad to kiss him goodbye when suddenly he said, 'Milly,' out loud.

Mam didn't twig to it straight away, she kept on

rearranging his pillow and putting the bananas where he could reach. Then her hands stopped suddenly in mid-air. 'You what?' she said. 'Ray, what did you say?'

Dad waited a while to get himself sorted and then said, 'Milly,' again, and, 'Milly glove.'

'You said, "Milly"!' Mam said. 'That's wonderful, Ray!' and she gave him a great big smacking kiss and then put her face at the side of his neck so you couldn't see it for a time. When she came up her face was red and her eyes looked funny, sort of pink and bright. Then she thumped at his pillow all over again and said, 'What's this glove? Have you lost something, Ray?'

And Dad said again, dead loud and clear, '*Glove*, Milly! Milly glove!'

There was a gap while we sat and looked at each other. You could hear the hospital going on, people shouting and the trundle of wheels and someone nearby having a cough.

Then the lady visiting at the next bed said, 'Ducky, I think he means to say "love".'

It was quite a bit later when we all got out, and by then it was dark. Dark and clear. You could see the stars again and the wind had dropped so our feet sounded loud and echoey.

We were chatting about what we'd have for tea – at least, I was, though Maddy was quiet. She's often quiet because Chrissy's so sharp and Mam goes nattering on all the time.

Now Mam kept saying, 'Milly glove,' as if it was some kind of miracle she was scared might disappear.

When we got home we had bacon for tea and then Mam got a list of people out. She said, 'These folks are all good for fifty pence, and count me in, that's fifty more.'

'There's Mr Pidgeon from next door,' I said. 'He says he's good for fifty too.'

'Coo!' said Maddy. 'You can put me down.'

'And me I s'pose,' our Chrissy said.

Later still I went round to Ben's. 'You can't stay long,' his mam said to me, 'he's to go to bed early with his chest.'

Ben was outside with the newts in the shed and I showed him the paper with the names on it. 'Good on yer, mate,' he said, grinning hard. Then he took the paper out of my hand and carefully showed it to the newts. 'See here,' he said to them, very soft, 'all these people put their money on you. That means you all got to run a good race. No going slow, right? Or we'll be up the spout.'

After that we had a go with the newts, and maybe the paper worked on them because they ran real fast, even Linda who's slow, and I was getting a feel for tickling their tails.

It was dark when I was starting to leave and Ben said, looking at my face, 'Barker got you then, did he, mate? You'll have to fix 'im good and proper – see here, if you like, I could send *my* mam round.'

'S'all right,' I said. 'I don't care much. Got other stuff to think about, right?'

And Ben put his hand on my arm real kindly and said, 'Well, mate, I reckon he'll get you again.'

I was in bed before I thought of Deep until my head ached with the thinking. I had the notion he wasn't dead yet, because if he was I was certain I would know. And nor was he properly alive. It seemed to me that Deep had gone way beyond dreaming to a place I couldn't reach and all I could do was wait, and watch.

I nearly went to sleep thinking about Deep but in the end I didn't. I thought about Barker instead. I wasn't scared of him like I had been before but I was fed up with having to see to him. And tomorrow he'd be looking for me. He and his mates would find me again. Maybe they would beat me up but, worse than that, they would tell everyone about our Chrissy and what she did. And that was worse, a *lot,* lot worse, than getting beaten up.

21
The big surprise

I went to school next day with my hands in my pockets, not walking fast and not walking slow. Other kids ran past laughing and yelling but the cloud in my head that was Deep was making me want to go to sleep, which was funny because I didn't feel sleepy. I was hearing things and seeing things but they weren't as clear as they were before; something was pulling me down and down, so my head was fuzzy and even my heart was beating slower.

I'm nearly *at* the school gate before Barker arrives. He comes up in front of me so I can't get past. His mates are there but they're hanging back and I can't be *bothered* with Barker again.

I decide to just stay where I am, and Barker stands there and he's grinnng at me. And I'm waiting for him to wallop me one. A moment goes past, and then another, and Barker's still there, saying nothing, but not letting me get past him, either.

In the end I say, 'Wotcher want?'

And Barker comes up to me, real close, and says, 'That your sister yesterday?'

And I say, 'Yes. What's it to you?'

And Barker goes, 'What's her name?'

And I go, 'Mind yer own business, Barker.'

Then Barker says, 'She got a boyfriend, d'you know?'

And I say, 'Eh? What d'you mean?'

And Barker says, 'D'you know what she thinks of me? Did she say anything – you know – after the fight?'

'Like what?' I say. 'I don't get you, right?'

After that I make to walk on past him, and it's then that something really strange happens. Barker comes and puts his arm round me. It goes over my shoulders like a heavy weight and out of the corner of my eye I can see his hand dangling down my arm. And I'm still unsure and half waiting for the beating. We're walking along the pavement together with me all stiff and awkward-feeling and Barker acting as if we were mates.

But then an even *stranger* thing happens. Barker says, 'I gotta note. You give it to your sister, right? Wasser name, then?'

And I say, 'Chrissy.'

So Barker's face goes all soft and gooey, and he says, 'Chrissy, OK. You give her that note – and listen, Jimbo – I'm your mate, now, right? Anyone gives you hassle again, you tell me and I'll sort 'em, right?'

That's when I cottoned what was to do: Barker fancied my sister, Chrissy! It beat me how anyone could fancy her! I mean, she's OK and all that, she's got her ducks in a row, but she's a mouth on her so sharp it'll cut. I mean – Chrissy and Barker!

I never said anything. Instead, my head went down on my chest and I kept very quiet so as not to upset things while I carried on thinking extra hard.

I thought that Chrissy would laugh herself silly at Barker sending her a soppy note. And if Barker cottoned that she didn't like him, he'd turn on me like he did before, only worse than ever, probably. So I said to him as quick as a flash, 'I'll give her your note, soon as I get home.'

Barker takes his arm away after that and slaps my back too hard, 'Right then, mate, you mind what I said. You get hassle: you tell me!'

At break he comes up to me again, 'How you doing, Jimbo, me old mate?'

Which makes Ben ask, 'How come you're friendly with *him* all at once?'

And that nearly made me tell him a lie, like, oh, we had a set-to on the way to school. I reckon he knows a thing or two now. Only I didn't, because for a start Ben wouldn't believe me if I did, and for another start I thought that he might help me out. So I told him what happened and he gave this laugh – *harrgh – harrgh* – that was more like a snort and said, 'No offence, mate, but *Chrissy*, harrgh!'

If it hadn't been Ben I might have biffed him one, but you don't go socking another wimp, so I folded my arms and waited a bit, and when he finished his laugh Ben straightened his scarf and said, 'I reckon you might have a problem there, mate. Your Chrissy don't like him, is that right?'

'You got it in one.'

'Well then, this is what you should do. You should open the note and read it, right? Then reply to it like you was Chrissy. Don't say stuff to put him off, but keep him hanging about, you know? That way you got a chance to get sorted. If you don't . . . well then, mate . . . I wouldn't want to be you.'

The bell went then and the rest of the day went past real slow. When school was finished I went round to see Dad.

Past the harbour entry I could see some men with cameras slung round their necks just standing about and doing nothing. I nearly went down to stand with them but I could see the water, choppy and black and empty looking. And I knew they wouldn't see Deep that day. I knew as well that it was likely *I* wouldn't see him again until he was dead and his body washed up. But right then there was this terrible waiting like you get before something bad's going to happen, a waiting that makes your whole body hurt.

When I arrived at the hospital it was raining. The lights were all on and outside the windows it was a mucky grey, streaked with rain running down the glass. Dad's chair was empty and so was his bed, smoothed down tight with the covers pulled up, and I made to go off down the ward to the therapy room with the plastic cups.

But all of a sudden I saw our dad.

He was walking down the ward – not on his own, there was a nurse with him holding on to an arm, and a stick was clenched in his good left hand. But Dad was concentrating really hard, putting down one foot and then another, stopping now and then to get back his puff and then slowly walking on again. Dad was concentrating so hard that he didn't see me standing there or the amazed expression on my face at seeing him back up on his feet.

When he came near me he stopped where he was and looked up, puzzled, before his face cleared.

'Smurffit bun!' he said, and wobbled a bit so the nurse had to grab at him to keep still.

I said, 'Smurffit,' back, still staring at him, then, 'You can walk, Dad, that's great! Does Mam know yet? Shall I tell her, like, or let her find out? Honest, Dad, I'm that pleased for you – I expect you'll be home soon, now you can walk.'

The nurse who was with him smiled at that and helped Dad back towards his chair, 'He's a way to go yet, pet, but he's doing well, and that can happen when you've had a stroke. A part of your brain can get better quickly, it's mainly a case of wait and see. And I reckon your dad's one of the lucky ones – he's getting better all on his own.'

She sat Dad down on the chair near his bed and I sat down next to him and took his hand.

The nurse said, 'Don't you stay too long now, chick, he'll tire much faster than usual today – but I'll tell you one thing – you do him good. He's a smashing family and that's for sure.'

When she'd gone I started to tell Dad things, all about me and Barker and school, and Dad was nodding and quirking his face and saying, 'Bimbly' and 'clobber' and 'Bimbly glove' and once, even 'I know' loud and clear, but I didn't catch on to that at first, and when I *did* catch on I had an idea.

It came to me that I was telling Dad all different things about me and Barker and school and Ben, but that none of it really mattered somehow. Because every word I spoke to him was really telling Dad about me, Jimmy Wilson, and that Dad was beginning to understand.

When I thought that I went quiet a bit and looked out the window at the wet grey sky. Then I looked back at Dad, who'd fallen asleep with his hair flopped down and his chin on his chest. I went away soon afterwards, so as to let Dad have his sleep, and took the quickest way back home.

There was nobody in and I couldn't seem to settle myself down. It felt like I was looking for something to show how we all used to be, instead of how we were right now.

A lot later on our mam came in and I said before she'd

even took off her coat, 'Dad can walk! Did you know he could? I seen him do it! Down the ward he came, easy as *that*!'

And Mam said, 'I know, Jimmy, I saw him at dinner, he just needs practice to get himself going.'

Then Chrissy came in and Madeline, too, so the ghosts in my head were chased out of sight and Mam said, 'Sausages! What about that? We'll have sausage 'n' chips to celebrate, and then some pears I got cut-price. Comice they are, a bit late, true, but the flavour's still good and there won't be many more.'

Afterwards I went upstairs and read Barker's note. It said:

> *I think your fantastick!!! Luvely hair and that*
> *youve got. What about us going out??? How come youve got*
> *a bruther like that??*
>
> *Barker*

I decided to do what Ben had said. I got out my pencil and some paper I found, and then I sat on my bed to have a think. And I'm telling you, I had to think real hard, because I'm not one to go writing much, but this is what I finally put:

> *Dear Barker,*
> *Got your note Im having a think. Thanks a lot for my hair and that.*
>
> *Chrissy*

* * *

I reckoned as that would keep him happy, but after I wrote it I felt extra tired.

Then Deep came swimming into my head like he was some kind of invisible thought-wave running silently between me and him.

It seemed to me that being a part of Deep's wild self was changing the way I dreamed. Now I could dream about being happy because of who I was instead of wishing I was someone else. And I didn't mind so much about Barker because there was other stuff more important to mind.

22
A change for the good

I set off to school early the next day, mainly because the news was on and I didn't want to hear about Deep. Deep's coming death was like a private place inside me that I wanted to *keep* private, not because I was scared of it but because when Deep died he would have broken free, and the wild part of me that was Deep wanted to break free with him and never come back.

I got to school as fast as I could and leant on a wall with my hands in my pockets and my collar up against the cold. The note to Barker was in my pocket and right then I felt like chucking it, just ripping it up and chucking it out, watching the bits float off in the wind. Next to Deep, Barker seemed small and stupid. And *after* Deep nothing would ever be the same again.

Suddenly the other kids disappeared and Barker was right in front of me. 'How ya doing?' he said, punching my shoulder. He was wearing knitted gloves without any fingers and a dark green balaclava.

'OK,' I said, 'I got you this.' I fished in my pocket and pulled out the note and stuck it in his woolly paw. Then I made a movement to walk away and Barker said,

'Hang about – I've not done yet.'

He read the note and I was stood like an idiot watching him. When he'd read it he stood still for a minute, just staring and staring with his little pink eyes until my heart gave a thump and jumped into my throat.

See, I thought Barker must have twigged what was what because of the wonky writing, or else the note was too short and not sloppy enough and that was how he'd found me out. But after another minute's hard staring he said, 'She's thinking, right?'

I shrugged.

'She's thinking all about me, right? She say anything? Like *what* she thought? She going to write again, or what?'

'Dunno. I could ask her, I s'ppose.'

'Yeah. Right. Hold on a mo. She liked what I put to her in the note. Maybe I'll write her another one. Yeah. I'll catch you up later, right, Jimbo?'

At break-time Ben said, 'Got something to show you – just the two of us, in private, mind.'

We went down the alley behind the school. 'What's up?' I said, and I was getting cold.

Ben reached in his bag and pulled out some paper. 'Made these up for us yesterday. What d'you think? Are they good or what? I thought as how we'd stick 'em up – you know, on walls and that where people can see. But it's a secret until we do it, right? Don't want anyone pinching 'em.'

The papers Ben gave me were coloured posters telling folks when the newt race was. They said:

GRAND NEWT RACE!!

FRIDAY

Best of Five

COME ALONG!

5.30

at

40 Beswick Road

WINNER GETS CERTIFICATE & PHOTO OF

WINNING NEWT

(to follow)

'Does your mam know about it?' I said.

'Course she does – and any road up, our mam's all right, she don't go making trouble for me.'

'Yeah. Well then. I think they're dead good.'

'You don't think they're not bright enough?' Ben sounded anxious and I gave a shrug.

'Nah. Dead right, if you were to ask me. I'll get Mam to

put one in Baverstock's where people can see it who've had a bet. What are you going to do with the rest?'

'One up in school if Miss Gray says so. One up in the newsagent's, and one on the tree at the end of our road.'

'Great. Brilliant. Good thinking, Ben. Can we go back now? I'm getting cold.'

Ben looked a bit hurt but he packed the posters up again and we went back into the main playground. Then at dinner I heard him chat to Miss Gray.

'Got these posters. What d'you think? Are the colours bright enough for the punters to see?'

And Miss Gray saying, 'My word, Ben, how clever you are. These posters are smashing, we'll have one in school.'

And Ben saying, 'Ta,' and heaving them up and tucking the end of his scarf in his trousers while Miss Gray fixed him with a soppy smile.

Before we went home Ben gave one to me. 'Keep it clean, right? And make sure to put it where people can see. And that newt on it, it's a common grey, only it's got more orange because it's male, OK? Just in case anyone wants to know.'

On top of the poster Ben had drawn a newt and coloured it in with waxy crayons. I showed it to Mam when I took it in, and she said, 'Blow me! That Ben's a clever lad – and lovely with it, if you were to ask me.'

Which made me give Mam a sideways look, because I

don't get this about Ben at all – I mean, what's so special about him all at once? No one ever says that about me.

'I'll put it up in the window, our Jim – my mates'll be tickled when they see it there. They'll all be coming along, you know, so make sure them newts is in fighting form.'

Mam put the poster up on the wall next to a sign that said *Frying Tomatoes* and another saying *Brussel Tops 18p*. 'There now,' she said, 'that'll draw some interest – I might even get Baverstock to bet fifty pence!'

I should have gone on then to see our dad, but I didn't – not straight away – because when I came out the shop Barker was there, leaning on a lamppost with his hands in his pockets and looking around impatiently. My heart gave this flip like it turned in my chest. I was waiting for Barker to say something, like, what d'you mean writing notes to me?' and follow it up with a fist to my nose. But all he did was shift from the lamppost and saunter over nonchalantly.

'Got this note for your Chrissy,' he said. 'Give it to her soon as you can. I'll be waiting, right? Till I hear from her.' Then he gave me a wink and slouched away.

After that I *did* go off to see Dad but for once I went round by the Scruff. Just for a while I stood close to the trees and listened to the blood bumping in my head. Then I made myself begin to think of Deep. Of Deep not being there, ever again, not even in a foreign sea.

It came to me then that I wasn't especially sad any more.

The part of me that was inside Deep knew that I would be going soon, and that when I went I would be free again. I gave this sigh, and with the sigh I felt light and giddy, like a weight had gone from off my skull. The houses and the estuary and the skeleton trees seemed suddenly a long way off; a hundred, thousand miles away. Slowly I began to walk on again. My hands were cold but I didn't notice, then the sun went in and it began to rain.

Later I was on the ward with Dad and we'd already said 'smurffit' and 'thrump' and I was thinking to tell him about the newts – about the posters and the date and that. I even thought as Dad might come, but tried not to wish for it too hard in case the wishing put a curse on it.

We were chuntering to each other back and forth and not saying a lot of anything much, when suddenly Dad took a hold of my hand and said, 'Jimmy,' as loud and as clear as I'm telling you. And before I could answer he said something else, 'Good boy, Jimmy. You're doing fine.'

At least, I'm nearly sure that's what he said, except it came out as, 'Goo oy, Jim. Ordon vine.'

When I heard Dad say that I bent right over to tie my laces and to have a cough. Then I came back up and said, 'You're not bad yourself,' and after that we chatted on.

I told Dad about the newt race then, and Dad chatted back with real words. Not always the right ones in the right order but you could tell what it was he wanted to say. Dad said, 'Nooot ace,' and 'Flannel' instead of saying 'Friday'. He talked like he was learning a foreign language or a code that you had to work out for yourself. And somehow that was almost better than before, as if we were *really* talking together, maybe for the very first time.

I left the ward just as Madeline came, clutching a jigsaw and a bunch of chrysanths. 'Hey-up, our Jim,' she said over the flowers. 'Dad OK then? You giving him lip?'

And I said, 'He's getting tired, I shouldn't stay too long,' and that made me feel dead sensible, as if I was suddenly all grown-up.

But Madeline said, 'You're a funny thing, Jimmy. Just hark at you! Real quaint you are.'

And the nurse said, 'Toodle-oo, then, Jimmy. Go straight home,' like she thought I was still a little kid.

I went off home and I was feeling OK. A blurry moon was coming out and I was walking along looking up at it, but instead of seeing the man in the moon I kept on seeing our dad's face. It made me think that something had changed and that most likely it was a change for the good.

Later on I was lying in bed when suddenly a new thought came: the newt race was going to take place soon, and what would happen if it failed?

23
The greenhouse

This is what Barker wrote in his second note to Chrissy:

Dear Chrissy,
Have you thorght yet? You could meet me tomorrow if you like. If not we could meet Satday. I still like your hair.
Barker

And this is what I wrote back:

Dear Barker,
Thanks again about my hair. Can't meet you. Got stuff to do. Think your OK and that.
Chrissy

That was on Thursday, and I went downstairs with it in my pocket and sat at the kitchen table. Chrissy was there, spooning cornflakes, and she gave me a look like she'd had a thought, and said, 'That big kid still bothering you?'

'Nah,' I said and shrugged nonchalantly, and would have gone on eating if she hadn't said,

'Only I keep on seeing him hanging about. He was outside the house yesterday tea-time, and later I saw him up the road.'

'Well,' I said, and I put down my spoon, 'he don't bother me. I can sort him out. Maybe he knows someone down here.'

'And maybe he don't! Listen, our Jim, I won't have him going bothering you. You get any trouble, you tell me.'

And that's another thing about being a wimp, people either want to beat you up or they want to look after you all the time. Why can't they just leave you alone?

When Chrissy finished talking our mam came in and the telephone rang, both at the same time. Mam said, 'Don't you leave without those apples. Baverstock sold 'em to me cheap – they've a bit of a bruise on them if you look.'

And the telephone voice said, 'Mrs Wilson? Katy Morgan here. I've just heard about Ray and I'm so sorry. Tell him his job'll always be there, only – he does my kitchen once a month, just a straightforward clean to freshen it up, and I wondered . . . d'you know anyone else who could do it for me? Just temporarily, to help me out? Give me a ring if you know someone. And give my love to Ray, if you will . . .'

When the voice finished nobody said anything but you

had the feeling that the telephone ringing just then had set a bell ringing in all our minds. Almost as if up until then we'd been listening to the same piece of news but we'd never really heard it before.

Then Mam said slowly, like she'd just thought of it, 'I don't know how much your dad will recover – if he'll ever be able to clean again.'

And Chrissy said, 'I could do Mrs Morgan on Saturday. Honest, Mam, I don't mind that at all.'

And Madeline said, 'I could do someone after school. Just to keep things ticking over for him.'

Mam didn't reply to either of them. Instead she sat there with her chin on her hands, and you could tell that she was thinking about having to stop at Baverstock's for ever and Dad not being able to work like he had and about us not having any money to spend.

Ordinarily we never bothered about that because we mainly enjoyed things that didn't cost much, like going out for picnics up Billicrank Hill or having a bonfire on the Scruff or going on our bikes to Castle Down. It was only now it struck me that everything might change. That instead of having Dad to look after us, we might have to look after him. And not just for a week or two, but maybe for ever when he came home.

Then Chrissy said, 'Oh, Mam, what will we do?'

I was sat at the table staring down at my plate while I

tried not to think about what might happen, such as all Dad's customers going somewhere else and Dad on his own in a chair all day.

Madeline said, 'We'll all do what we can, our Mam.'

Which seemed to make Mam suddenly brisk. She got up from the table and gathered some dishes and said, 'Right, for a start you can all of you get off to school – and take those apples with you, now, we can't go wasting stuff like that. And don't go thinking about what I just said. Something will turn up to sort us all out, so don't go worrying yourselves about it.'

After that we all went off to school. Chrissy didn't try to come with me, she just slung her backpack over her shoulders and stamped off down the empty street. I walked slowly on my own and I was nearly there when Barker came up. I never actually heard him come – I was too busy thinking about our Dad – but suddenly I got this punch in my back and Barker was there in his dark blue parka, grinning all over his face at me.

'Gotta note, have you?' he said.

And something happened I hadn't planned. His hand was out in its woolly glove and I'd nearly put the note in it when suddenly I changed my mind. I tore it up very slowly and then put the pieces back in my pocket and said, 'Chrissy don't like you after all. She says you're trouble and she'll sort you out.'

Then I waited while Barker had a think. If you watched him you could see him thinking because his face went blank, and then it went mean, and then it cleared all at once and he gave this laugh and slapped me hard on the shoulder again and said, 'Oh yeah! Great! I like that, right? I mean your Chrissy sorting me out!'

He sauntered away with his arm round the shoulders of one of his mates, and you could hear him laughing while they went.

Then Ben came up and said, 'You've cracked it, mate. You told him straight. It's up to him now to do what he likes – and maybe your Chrissy *will* sort 'im out!'

The day went past real slow after that and I could see Barker looking my way now and then but he never came up and nothing got said. Then Miss Gray put the poster up in the hall, so kids kept going up to Ben and saying, 'Fancy that! Can you race a newt? And can I come over and watch 'em tomorrow, if I give you a bet for say, twenty pence?' Which meant Ben got to talk about newts all the time *and* he had this great long list of money that all the kids had pledged.

At tea-time I went straight round to see Mam and her poster was still up on Baverstock's door. 'Hey-up, our Jimmy,' she said when I went in. 'This here poster's caused quite a stir. Everyone's asking after you – you're that popular I can scarce keep up – and they're all looking forward to a really good do!'

Then she came out from behind the counter and leant down and whispered in my ear, 'Baverstock's promised to cough up a fiver tomorrow if the race goes off the way you reckon it will.'

After that she stood back and tapped her chin and looked as if she was thinking hard. Then she clicked her fingers and said all at once, 'Nuts! That's right! Hang on a sec. We got these brazils in fresh today and they're that good and snappy, they're a pleasure to eat! Here, take these to your dad, Jimmy, and give a few to the bloke next door.'

I went outside with the nuts in a bag and set off for the hospital through the town. It was lighter than it had been before; there was still some sun showing through the clouds and in gardens you could see bulbs coming up, crocuses and daffodils and stuff like that, the kind of flowers we had at home. That made me think of a thing Dad had said, about how much he liked to be outside: 'If I'd been able to go off to college, our Jim, I'd have been a gardener and worked outside.' At home folks come and peer over the hedge. You can hear them chuntering on to each other:

'I wish old Ray'd come and do mine.'

Perhaps it was me remembering about Dad and his garden that made it happen, but when I got to the hospital Dad wasn't there. His jumper was gone from the back of his chair and his shoes were missing from under the bed. I was standing looking flummoxed when the lady visiting at the next bed said, 'He's in the greenhouse today, darling. Your dad – what a man! I'm telling you, son, he's no need to work with all them plants, he's a rose, you ask me, among the thorns!'

I gave her the nuts when she said that and she laughed out loud, 'Heh heh heh,' and said, 'Your mam – she's sweet as a nut herself.'

After that I went off down the ward and into the greenhouse that stuck out at the end. A nurse was in there and so was Dad, and the nurse said, 'Hello, young Jimmy – come over here. Look at your dad and what he can do – my word, he's quick! And neat – blow me! I couldn't do this job half so well, even with my two good hands!'

Dad was sitting down at a wooden bench and he was planting seedlings out in a box. He was using his good left hand to do it and the way he worked was quick and gentle, so none of the seedlings got messed up.

He hardly looked up when he heard me come in, he just said, 'Yo, Yimbly,' and carried on working, digging around with the end of a pencil and pricking out the tiny plants.

And I expect I was disappointed by that. See, I'd got used to having Dad to myself. So I hung around and got fed up, and I reckon Dad picked up on it because he suddenly stopped what he was doing. He put his good hand down on the table very slowly and carefully, then looked at me with his face quirked up. For a while we neither of us spoke, then

Dad said, 'Yimbly elp. Gooyad, Yim.' He shuffled further up on the bench and I sat myself down next to him. Then we carried on planting seedlings out and neither of us spoke again.

We worked on until the glass roof went dark and you could see stars coming out in the coal-black sky, and somehow the not-speaking was OK then, like words would have gone and messed things up and we were talking louder than we did with words.

I left Dad late and went home for my tea (some beans on toast) and Mam and the girls were already in. We were all sitting round the table again, chatting together about this and that, everything fine and normal-seeming. But I had this feeling of stuff held back.

I finished my tea and went upstairs – and I'll tell you something that likely sounds wrong: I wasn't worried about Dad at all. Maybe it was spring coming, or being with Dad and doing the plants, but that lightness I got the day before when I thought about Deep and his breaking free – that was still with me. My head felt light and clear as air and I went to sleep with it like that.

Then I dreamt of Dad and Deep together, swimming along in the clear blue sea, and I reckon I probably laughed in my dream.

After that I dreamt about the newts and I was urging them on and tickling their tails. They were bombing along, no trouble at all and then, abruptly, I was awake. It was seven o'clock. It was Friday the 14th.

It was the day we were running the Great Newt Race.

24
'Good old Ben'

I still wasn't thinking about Deep on Friday – or not properly, anyway. He was *in* my mind, if you understand me, like he was a piece of my own brain, but he wasn't *on* it. Mam and the girls didn't put the radio on for the news, either, nor did they talk about Deep, the way they didn't talk about Dad being poorly and maybe not ever working again. Only every so often I saw them look at me. Just a quick look, there – *flick* – and away again, as if they were sorry for me, like they knew something had happened to Deep but weren't ever going to tell me.

They talked about the Great Newt Race. What I got was plenty of lip:

'Well, our Jimmy, you're looking sharp – shall I get some Brylcreem to put on your hair?'

'I've got a checky jacket upstairs – bit too big in the shoulders, though.'

'I hope you're off out with them newts today – to give 'em a trot, like, over the downs.'

Even Mam joined in with it. 'I hope each newt has its own colour, Jimmy, and you're posting the running order up.'

Not that I cared much about all that, because sisters always go twittering on. It's what they do, right? It makes them happy, that's what I reckon, thinking up smart things to say to you.

I got to school early and Ben came up. He was wearing a new scarf his mam had knitted in a swirly pattern of pinks and blues. 'See here,' he said when he got close enough, 'about later on. We'll have five races, right? One bet covers all of them and whichever newt wins the most races, that's the one that wins the prize. And these here, they're certificates, to tell folks that their newt got first place. I done about ten, that should be enough, and I'll have me camera there, OK? I'll take some snaps of the winning newt and maybe some of the lucky winners. We'll send 'em off to folks later on. Is there anything else you can think of to do?'

I said, 'Well . . .'

And Ben said, 'Right! Good thinking, mate. We'll put a few flags up round the shed and Mam's getting me a whistle today – got to set them off right, yeah? And Mam says she'll make pots of tea and that, and maybe some biscuits if there's not too many folks.'

It was a mystery to me how Ben could think of so many things all at the same time, and how the other kids could think he was brilliant now and not the Ben they usually ignored. See, the others had already swum ten lengths or walked twelve miles or climbed something, and you'd think they might have laughed at him.

When we went into school there were newts everywhere. Ben's poster was still up in the hall and another was up on the classroom wall. Then Miss Gray said we had to do newts for art and she borrowed Ben's books and read bits out.

After we finished doing art Miss Gray sent Ben round the room looking at all our pictures. He got to pick the best ones out and Miss Gray put them up around the school.

And I reckon that Ben was enjoying himself, because all the time stuff was going on he was grinning and grinning and wiping his nose and telling kids things they didn't want to know, like how newts hibernate in winter and bury themselves in soil or rocks; about how they play dead if they feel like it and lay their eggs round special plants. Ben was behaving as if he was popular, right, and not a wimp the same as me. I was nearly ready to explode at him, to say stuff like, 'Well, pardon *me*! I expect you think you're brilliant now!' But something stopped me in the nick of time.

Probably it was thinking about Dad sitting under the starry glass planting seedlings and enjoying himself. Or this sudden picture I got of Deep, quiet and still, lying in the mud of the estuary while the wind blew in the empty trees and the sun shone high above. I didn't even mind when Barker came up and said, 'Your Chrissy be at the race later on?'

I shrugged at him and said, 'Dunno,' and that made Barker slap my shoulder and say,

'Cheers then, mate,' before he walked off.

After school I went home with Ben, but before we could get there some more kids came up. They were slapping Ben's back and saying, 'See you soon, right?' and 'Good old Ben. Be round later on.'

When we got to Ben's house his mam was waiting on the front door step, and as soon as we came up she said, 'Ben, you'd better have your tea now, pet. There's some sandwiches and a chocolate sponge with icing on the way you like – it'll do you until a bit later on. When you've had a sit we'll do the flags and you can help me get the table out.'

And I've this to say about Ben's mam: her sponge cake's brilliant! She puts chocolate inside!

After we'd had our tea we went outside to put flags up between the shed and the house, and me and his mam were standing on chairs while Ben said, 'Up a bit, down a bit. That's OK,' and, 'That needs to go just a *bit* further right.'

There was a trestle table to race the newts on and Ben had made separate lanes for each of them out of thin strips of coloured ribbon I'd borrowed from Baverstock's on the quiet. The finishing post was a long thin twig and Ben had even made a black and white flag to sweep down at the end of the race.

We'd hardly finished when people came through the gate. First there were some kids from school, giggling and scuffling and shoving each other, then Miss Gray in a really smart coat. Mam came along next with Aunty Mavis, beaming and winking and waving at me, and Mr Pidgeon came all on his own. When Mam saw Mr Pidgeon she said, 'How-do, Reg!'

'Very well, thanks. How's Mr Wilson? I expect he'll be back at Business soon?'

For a short moment I saw something like a thin dark shadow skim over Mam's eyes, but all she said was, 'Not yet-a-while, Reg, but thank you for asking all the same.'

Chrissy and Madeline came after that but I was nearly too busy to talk to them because I was going around collecting the money. I had to go right in amongst the crowd and find out what they were going to pledge, then put their money in a red cloth bag and tick their names from off the list. By then all the ladies from Baverstock's were there, laughing and drinking tea from a flask and eating potted meat sandwiches. They kept coming up and pinching my chin and saying stuff like, 'If I were twenty years younger I'd race after *you*!'

At half past five the races began. Ben and me were to be at the front and his mam was at the finishing line. Miss Gray was in the middle to umpire, so we all of us knew where we had to stand. And then Ben came out with the box of newts.

He put them down on the table very carefully, while everyone near by went 'Shushh!' so in the end it was dead still and quiet. Even the wind had stopped for once, and Ben took the newts out one at a time and put them down on the table top. You could have heard a pin drop. Then I heard a kid say, 'I don't fancy yours!'

And that made everyone start shouting out:

'Which one's Linda?'

'Mine's Santa, right?'

'That one with the long legs, that's Dandy, OK?'

'Beano's not looking in top form – can I swap to Puddle or is it too late?'

People were making all that noise and I almost didn't see Barker arrive. Then I clocked him coming round the side of the house and scanning the crowd for where Chrissy was.

At the very same moment Ben said loudly, 'Quiet everyone! I'm going to count to three. Best of five races. Good luck to you all!'

After that I flexed my fingers hard, ready to tickle the newts' long tails while the people watching went quiet again. I heard Ben say, 'Are you ready, mate?' then draw a deep breath to steady himself. For a second nothing happened at all, then Ben said, 'Right-ho: one, two, three, GO!' and he blew a loud blast on his new red whistle.

25
The great newt race

Ben kept up a commentary: 'That's Beano coming up on the outside. Behind him comes Dandy – he's going fine. Santa's not found his form just yet – oh yeah! Puddle's coming up behind Beano. I reckon he's going to overtake him!'

I was tickling Linda and Puddle and Cotton and Ben was tickling the rest of them, but I could hardly get old Cotton to run. He just stood there gently stretching his legs and flicking out his long black tongue. And that set some of the punters off:

'Come on, Cotton, get on with it!'

'Tickle harder – you're too kind to him!'

'Call that a runner? That's more like a snail!'

Everyone was shouting out and leaning forward over the table and giving out their best advice. Even Mr Pidgeon forgot himself and I heard him shout, 'Come on, Cotton! Show 'im the crop! He'll run fast then, you mark my words!'

Beano won the race outright and that made the other punters groan. 'That Beano – he should be 'andicapped. I reckon his legs are longer than most.'

The second race went on, and then the third. Beano won one, then Santa took over, just when we'd got him tagged as a loser. By the fourth race the score was Beano two, with Santa and Puddle scoring one each. Linda and Dandy were nowhere to be seen and Cotton had come in last every time.

When the fifth race came it went dead tense and quiet. The folks who'd backed Beano were puffing their chests and the ones who'd been and backed Puddle and Santa were hoping it might mean an extra race. But Ben acted like he was on his own. He turned his back on the audience and talked to his newts very soft and gentle while he tickled them under their wrinkly chins.

After that they were at the starting gate and me and Ben were arranging the line. Then Ben raised his hand for quiet again and blew his whistle for the very last time.

'Here comes Santa down the last straight – Beano's not very far behind. What's this? That's Cotton coming up! An outsider's taking over the run! Next comes Santa and then old Puddle, and Linda's in the inside lane – and, yes!! Santa's taken over the lead, so that's Santa and Cotton and Puddle next – and *wham*! Santa's been and gone over the line. Yes, folks, it's Santa who's won this time!'

Ben waved the black and white flag up and down in front

of the winning newt, and people hugged themselves and shouted and cheered, and there was a sudden flash from a camera bulb. A man from the *Evening Post* had come and was saying to Ben, 'Stand still, son. And hold the newt a bit higher up. Now, give us a smile – no *you* I mean, son, not the newt.'

After that more photographs got took and Ben's mam fetched the tea-pot out, and kids were coming up to me and saying stuff like, 'Do you do newts? Can I come and look? Have you got a shed with a tank like Ben's?'

I'd nearly forgotten that Barker was there, what with all the excitement and that, when suddenly I spotted him. He was talking to Chrissy behind a plant and I could see our Chrissy going red in the face. Then I saw Barker make a sudden move and give her cheek a very quick kiss. After that I saw Chrissy walloping him and Barker go staggering back from it with a hand clutched up to the side of his face. Next Barker looked round the garden for me, and strolled dead casually to where I was standing behind a giant holly bush.

He came up grinning and said to me, 'Your Chrissy said she never got no notes – but I reckon she likes me after all. I reckon she's just playing hard to get; else why would she sock me the way she did?' He laughed and went off swaggering, then Chrissy came up and she was still bright red.

'You been writing notes for me, Jimmy Wilson? I thought

you had, and I'm that flaming mad! I could murder you, Jimmy, honest I could, except that we're in company, like. Oh – bloaters to it, I don't much care – here, hang on a sec while I get me puff.' Chrissy took a step back to measure me up and then walloped *me* one over my ear!

Next I had some more chocolate cake and watched Miss Gray give certificates out: 'It gives me more pleasure than I can say . . .' Her next words were carried away by the breeze.

Later than that it was suddenly dark. The flags and the table were taken in and the newts were put back in the shed. Through the darkness you could see the backs of houses like rows of dirty piano keys. Most of the houses had orange lights on, and the lights made me think of the hospital and of Dad being in there on his own and missing all the fun we'd had.

I went home then to Mam and the girls, and later still we went to see Dad. He wasn't in the greenhouse when we arrived, he was sitting on the chair next to his bed, but you could tell where he'd been because of his nails. There was a black ring of earth running underneath them and you got this waft of green stuff growing. It was a scent like the scruff smells after rain, kind of soft but with a salty edge that made you think that if you touched it, it would feel like green silk in your hand.

If we'd been another family it's likely we'd have just sat quiet, but as it was we all talked at once. I was saying, '. . . So

Santa won, and you know what, Dad? Ben's Mam makes these smashing cakes!'

And Chrissy was saying, '. . . So I said to our Jimmy, "Did you send him notes?" and then I socked him one. Honest, Dad, I was that flaming mad when I found what he did, I couldn't hardly help myself . . .'

Madeline was having a good old moan: 'Nobody ever writes me notes. D'you think I'm pretty? Just a little bit, Dad?'

Mam was talking and holding his hand: 'Well, I went to see Baverstock after the race and he gave me five pounds just like *that*! I got these mangos for you as well. They've stones in them but they're full of juice. Maybe the nurse would peel you one?'

All in all it was all right that night. Even the thought of Deep silent and alone didn't stop me from being happy. Like I said, it seemed to me Deep's time had come and that was something I had got to know slowly, and with a pain like I'd never ever felt before. He was in my head where he'd always be but right then I could see something that nearly made me decide to stop fretting, most likely for good and all. What I saw was Dad being happy in spite of still being really ill, and it made me think, what if you could just *decide* to be happy? To always picture the best of things instead of the very worst?

When Dad got tired we all went home, very slowly, arm in arm. Clouds had wafted over the sky so you couldn't see the stars that night, but you had the notion of something bright waiting behind the drift of dark.

And I didn't look towards where Deep was, not even when I heard the wind whistling to me like the call of the sea.

Instead I pictured Deep as happy.

I pictured the very best for him.

26
Celebrities!

Come the next day I was down in the dumps. None of us looked too chipper at breakfast. Even Mam, who's always so cheerful and bright, hardly spoke to us. It made me wonder if what I had thought the day before about deciding to be happy wasn't right after all and you just had to get on with how things were. I even said something like that out loud, and Chrissy said in a fierce whisper, 'Shut up, Jimmy Wilson. Mam's worried stiff about Dad's work.'

Our Maddy gave me this vague, sad smile, and even though I thought it was mainly because she hadn't got any notes from lads, it still made me feel achey inside.

I got to school and I was early for once, and Miss Gray spotted me straight away. She'd just parked her car and was locking it up when she waved a hand to beckon me over. She said, 'Well, Jimmy Wilson, there's some good news for you!

Just you wait until a bit later on and *then* you'll get a big surprise!'

She wouldn't say any more after that but when Ben came up he was grinning again.

'How much money d'you reckon we took?' Ben was eating a gooey chocolate bar and his words came out all muffled up.

'Dunno,' I shrugged and kicked at a stone.

'Forty-eight pounds and twenty pence! That's most people having fifty p and a few late-comers at twenty p each. I reckon that's good, Jimbo me old mate, and it's done me newts good to get limbered up.'

'Yeah. Great. It went real well. How's old Cotton doing today?'

'He's disappointed, that's how he is. But I told 'im "Listen, it's only a race, we can't all win, that's how it is," but ol' Cotton, he's gone under a rock and won't come out again, even for me.'

'Maybe he could join the Wimps Club, right? That way he never need race again. Tell him that when you get home. Tell him we'll make him one of us.'

'Brilliant! Ta. I'll tell 'im that. He's highly strung, like Mam says about me. An invitation'll do 'im good.'

After that we went into school and it wasn't like school usually was, it was strange and exciting, just as if both of us were heroes for once. Kids kept coming up and saying stuff like, 'You're dead good, you are, with them newts. Can I have a go another time?' and, 'Fancy thinking of that to do! I only swam a few stupid lengths.'

I even got moaned at for being too loud, and Miss Gray doesn't usually bother with me. She shouted, 'Jimmy Wilson will you stop that rattle? Say what you've got to say later on.' And that made some kids roll their eyes at me like they did when one of their mates copped it, and someone even passed me a note. It said, *See you at break – don't forget. Got some cake me mam's give me.*

At half past ten we went into the hall while Mrs Potts played a marching tune on the piano. And then we sang:

> *Sing Hosanna! Sing Hosanna!*
> *Sing Hosanna to the King of kings . . .*

And all clapped too loud or not loud enough. Next the Head said, 'Sit down, everyone – Andrew Barker, that means you!' and she told us all off about making noise and about some litter she'd found outside. Then we sang another song and she talked about us having to be more polite. After that she stopped and cleared her throat.

We were all on the floor and we were looking at her and wondering what she was going to say, when suddenly she gave this smile and said, 'And now, children, some good news for you. Your efforts to help the children in Africa have raised over two hundred and fifty pounds! Give yourselves a clap for that. You deserve it – really – so clap away!'

For once Mrs Kershaw let us all clap loud and we clapped away until her hand went up. After that it went real quiet again, and she said, 'I'll tell you now who raised the most money through a really unusual effort of their own.

'The children who raised the most money were: BEN DELANEY AND JIMMY WILSON! Come up to the front, boys, and the rest of you give them a great big clap!'

I didn't catch on to what she said straight away, mainly because I was so surprised, and Ben had to give me a dig in the ribs and hiss at me out the side of his mouth, 'Come *on*, mate, quick. It's us she means!'

That's when I heard the other kids clapping and saying stuff like, 'Good old Ben!' and, 'Brilliant, Jimmy – my newt won!' At the side of the hall I could see Miss Gray nodding her head and smiling at me, and then we were up in front of the school and Mrs Kershaw was speaking out again.

'Your effort deserves a small reward for all the enterprise you have shown. Miss Gray has kindly made a plaque for you both to share. You can put it up on the classroom wall. Well done!'

We took the plaque and went back to our places with everyone clapping real loud again. After that we had another song, and then we all went back to our rooms.

Miss Gray said, 'Well done, both of you. Shall we put the

plaque up on the wall now? Everyone will want to look at it, but first let me read to you what it says.' She took the plaque away from us and put her spectacles on her nose. Then she read:

'This plaque is presented to
BEN DELANEY & JAMES WILSON
for
THE GREAT NEWT RACE
being
their efforts on behalf of
Dingwa Village School'

Ben said, 'That's great, that is, isn't it, Jim? My mam'll be dead proud of me!'

I heard what Ben said but I didn't reply. Instead, I looked out of the window at the wide blue sky and tried my best not to think about Deep.

But Deep was inside my mind again and I couldn't shut him out. Something was happening, I knew it was, because the way he was with me was different this time. He was trying to talk to me properly; he was sending out these low, soft vibes, wanting to say something really important, something I didn't want to hear because I was too afraid. Right then, when he needed me most, I was shutting Deep out as hard as I could. I was trying to make out he wasn't there.

See, I knew that something would happen soon, in spite of me not wanting it to, and it was knowing it that made me scared. Not because Deep was back again but because I knew that soon he would break my heart.

When I got home I felt jumpy and weird in spite of Mam and the girls being there. We were all of us sitting round the table and I was telling them about the plaque and that. Mam was saying, 'Well done, our Jim. You've a head on your shoulders, I'll say that for you. I reckon you get it from your dad.'

And Madeline was saying, 'Come here, chick, and have a hug. Then I'll give you some chocolate.'

Chrissy was saying, still humpy with me, 'Well! You managed to get *something* right! You're not a bad lad, Jimmy, when all's said and done.'

We were nattering backwards and forwards like that and not expecting company, when all of a sudden we heard these footsteps tapping along down the passage outside. As soon as we heard them we went quiet and still, then Mam said, 'Quick – shift the milk bottle, Jimmy!' at the same time as this shout went up:

'Yoo-hoo! Don't worry, it's only me. No need for you to take a fright!'

The door opened next and Aunty Mavis came in. She surged in on this great waft of scent, all out of breath and puffing hard but with a big red lipsticky smile on her face. As soon as she saw me she came right over and said, 'Well, our Jimmy – what a surprise! Quite a celebrity you are tonight!'

I guess I must have looked baffled then, because she gave this laugh and patted my face and then dived into the bag she carried and fished a piece of paper out. The paper was cut from the *Evening Post* and there was this picture of me and Ben and the newts, with a caption underneath that said, *Chocs away for Ben Delaney and Jimmy Wilson and the Great Newt Race*! Ben was grinning out from the page with a newt held up in front of his scarf, and I was staring like a rabbit with another newt clutched in my hand.

'Well I'm blowed,' our mam gave a laugh. 'We'll have to pay to speak to you soon!'

'You look like a halfwit in that, our Jim.' That was Chrissy speaking out.

'And I think he's *scrumptious*!' Aunty Mavis said.

It was after she said that I gave this gasp, because I realised that a strange thing had happened in our house again, and it was a thing that only ever happened when Aunty Mavis was there.

What I realised was: Aunty Mavis was a witch! Only not a bad witch who did wicked things; a witch who was really good and kind. Her big scented self seemed to fill the room; her fat white fingers unfolded the paper and great smacking kisses were planted all round. Even Chrissy seemed to relax and stop being humpy and cross with me. It was just as if Aunty Mavis really did have a happiness zapper gun that only worked when she was there. After she left it was like a spell being broken and us all going back to how we were, not good or bad but ordinary, just the same as everyone else.

Except that this time Aunty Mavis had another surprise.

After she'd got us all perked-up and laughing, and showed the photograph around and undone a cake she'd brought for us, she sat down at the table and loosened her coat. The coat fell away like a dark red cloak and showed a glittery necklace up. Aunty Mavis touched the necklace and sighed, then she took a hold of one of Mam's hands.

She said, 'There might be something our Ray can do – I mean when he's better than he is now, like.'

'Eh?' said Mam. 'What do you mean? Our Ray's a cleaner, that's what he does, although he might never clean again.'

When Mam said that her face went crumpled and sort of inward-looking.

Aunty Mavis gently patted her hand. 'That's what I'm trying to tell you, Milly. If Ray can't clean there's something else. There's this friend of mine, a kind of old flame. Well, this bloke owes me a favour or two, so I said to him, could he fix Ray up. He runs a nursery, you see, and that'd be right up our Ray's street.'

When Aunty Mavis finished speaking nothing happened

for a moment or two; we all just sat there while the clock ticked away and the letter box rattled in the wind. For a while I thought nothing *would* happen.

Then Mam said, 'A *nursery*? What do you mean, Mavis? A nursery would be brilliant, sure, but what could our Ray do in it?'

'He hasn't ever worked with nippers before – see, babies and that, they'll make him confused. Our dad don't know much about little kids.'

I said that and then went a bright steamy red because everyone started to laugh out loud. 'Trust you, our Jimmy! Fancy saying that! Harr harr harr, hee hee hee. Fancy not knowing what a nursery is! They do say there's one born every day!'

It was mostly Chrissy saying that, but everyone else had a good laugh too, and I very nearly got humpy myself until Aunty Mavis did her witch thing again.

'Sweetheart!' she said, and kissed my cheek and then rubbed the lipstick mark away. 'You're a rare one, you, I'm pleased to say. It's a gift you've got to make people laugh. You stay as you are, Jimmy, OK?'

Then Madeline said what a nursery was: 'It's a place for growing plants and that. You plant lots of seeds and prick them out and when they're ready you sell the big plants on.'

'And that's where Ray comes in again!' Aunty Mavis beamed across the table. 'He's that nimble with his good left hand, I reckon he'd be a dab at that – and so I told Michael – he's the fella I mentioned before – and *he* said, "Fine. Send him round to me when he's ready. I could do with a really careful bloke." '

After that the day couldn't get much better. We'd all finished eating our sandwiches but Mam got the Christmas sherry out and some lemonade she'd made herself from a bag of Baverstock's cut-price fruit. Then we cut the cake Aunty Mavis had brought and got out a record that Dad would have liked. This time it was 'Save the Last Dance for Me', and Mam and Aunty Mavis danced round the room while Chrissy and Madeline clapped and cheered.

It was only later that it went very quiet.

Aunty Mavis had gone back home and Madeline and Chrissy were watching the telly and chuntering on from time to time. Mam had gone round to see our Dad, and she said she wanted to go on her own. She went out the door still saying stuff like, 'Fancy! I mean! I can't believe it! Our Ray getting a job like that!'

And I went upstairs to my room.

But when I got there I felt peculiar. Not miserable or headachy but as if something was fizzing away very gently inside me. I felt like that night before you go on holiday, jumpy and excited and looking forward to it, but not really sure that you want to go.

I got into bed and put out the light, still with my head

feeling buzzy and strange. And I thought I wouldn't get to sleep. I thought I'd lie where I was and stare at the window with the moon behind it; a grey shape that was nearly lost under a bank of drifting clouds.

But instead, sleep came to me almost at once.

Only this sleep was like your imagination, full of strange pictures looming out of the gloom and a feeling like you were starting something: an adventure or a special journey, and you didn't know where it was going to end.

I slept on, dreaming, and then I woke up.

And I knew that Deep had woken me; that he was calling to me and I had to go.

27
Free at last

It was still pitch black when I opened my eyes. You couldn't even see the wardrobe in the corner of the room. I didn't know what time it was, but straight away I was wide awake and instead of feeling heavy I felt light as air. And I knew immediately that I'd been pulled awake. That Deep was calling and that he meant me to go to him.

I got out of bed and tugged on some clothes and never even thought about Mam and the girls; I just knew they wouldn't hear me because what was happening was special to me and nobody else was meant to hear.

Outside in the street the lamps were still lit. There was no one about apart from me and I could hear the blood inside my head pounding out like the noise of the sea surging: *boom boom boom.*

When I got to the harbour there was no sign of Deep. The water in front of me was thick and black as the night, and so silent you couldn't hear it swelling.

I stood on the wall and looked out over the estuary at the road bridge, still lit up like a ghostly ship. There were no cars or lorries trundling over it and you had the feeling that everything that moved was being held back, only not by people the way it was before; more as if the force of Deep's great mind had somehow stopped the whole world moving.

For a long time I stood on the edge of the water with my head singing and light as air.

And nothing happened.

Deep didn't appear.

He was in my head and he was in my bones; he was all around me like the air I breathed, it was just that I couldn't see him yet. I waited a while, and then longer than that, and while I waited dawn came up. First it was a finger of light, pointing over the silent water and then it was purple and pink and white, and you could see trees clearly on the other side.

I was watching the sky changing colour and listening to the first bird sing, when suddenly the water began to stir, very softly and gently at first, so you thought you were imagining it. There was just a ripple underneath the surface and a noise like a long, soft sigh coming out. The sigh ran through my head like wild music, so all I could hear was *ssi-ghh ssi-ighh ssi-ghh.*

Then the water rippled again and slowly, slowly Deep rose up at the same time as the sun flared out, firing him with a golden light. Deep rose from the water in a golden arc and hung there, huge and glittering. You could see his body in a sparking curve and the beautiful glittering sweep of his tail.

Deep hovered in the light in front of me, hardly moving himself at all. And I remembered that thing I read about whales:

Sperm whales have skin as thin as gold leaf.

It seemed to me that Deep was even more amazing than if he had just been made out of gold leaf. It seemed to me that he was all that I was, and all that I ever wanted to be.

I was thinking that, and watching Deep and wishing that I could go with him, when he slowly began to sink back down into the sparkling water. I saw him start to swim away, slowly at first, then faster and faster. He was a swift golden shape plunging through the bright waves, rising and falling, forging on. I saw him go past the railway bridge and out towards the open sea, and as he swam he grew thinner and thinner, until he was almost as thin as a whisp of gold leaf, until his glitter was a fading gleam, a spark caught in the eye of the sun, until at last he disappeared.

I saw Deep go.

And I was the only one who saw.

Free at last, the way I had wished for him through all the long, cold winter days.

'Deep!' I shouted silently. 'Good luck, Deep.'

After he left I turned away. I thought about Deep being true to himself, the way I had always wanted to be. Then I thought about Dad and the nursery; about Mam, and The Great Newt Race, and the girls. The amazing way things were working out.

Then slowly I made my way back home.